HAIR

EVERYTHING YOU EVER WANTED TO KNOW

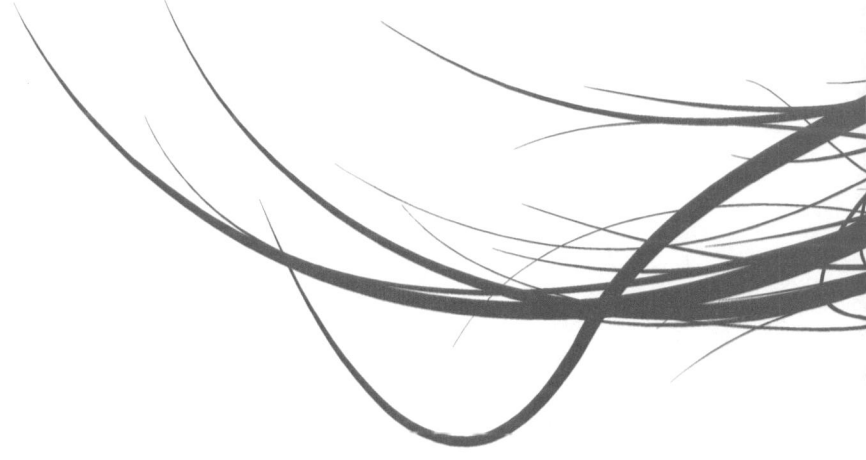

Dr Akshay Batra

BHMS, LTTS, AMP

President, The Trichological Society, London, UK
Managing Director, Dr Batras' Positive Health Clinic Pvt Ltd
Director, Dr Batra's B Perfect Clinics, India

HAIR

EVERYTHING YOU EVER WANTED TO KNOW

Dr Akshay Batra

BHMS, LTTS, AMP

President, The Trichological Society, London, UK
Managing Director, Dr Batras' Positive Health Clinic Pvt Ltd
Director, Dr Batra's B Perfect Clinics, India

EMBASSY BOOKS
www.embassybooks.in

EMBASSY BOOKS
120, Great Western Building,
Maharashtra Chamber of Commerce Lane, Fort,
Mumbai - 400 023, India.
www.embassybooks.in

© Dr Akshay Batra

HAIR: EVERYTHING YOU EVER WANTED TO KNOW

ISBN: 978-93-81860-33-5

First Published by Embassy Books 2012

DEDICATION

To my father, Dr Mukesh Batra, a visionary homeopath of international repute, healer to all... including statesmen, presidents, leaders and celebrities; best-selling author, photographer, musician, extraordinary human being and a great source of inspiration to me.

... My mother, Nalini Batra, for all her love and affection.

... And, my son, Hriman, whose electrifying enthusiasm to know the why, how and what of everything, eggs me on to (re)discover things with a child-like new perspective and also look at life without glasses.

ACKNOWLEDGEMENTS

I would like to acknowledge the following people for their contribution to this work: Rajgopal Nidamboor, Dr Sapna Punjabi-Giri, Dr Tejal Ajmera-Patel and Ambika Shukla.

Barry Stevens, for his passion and commitment to trichology; for placing it on a strong, scientific foundation, and for his belief in me.

My publisher, Sohin Lakhani, for his passion and keen interest in the project.

I have been fortunate to work with my devoted medical and support staff at Dr Batra's Clinics and B Perfect Clinics, and able to witness first-hand the excellent holistic workings of trichology and homeopathy in patients with hair loss.

I thank them, and, above all, my patients, for having placed their continued confidence in me.

This book is not just my book; it is your book too.

— Dr Akshay Batra

CONTENTS

SECTION IV: *MANAGEMENT OF HAIR PROBLEMS*

SECTION V: *HAIRSTYLE TIPS, DIET, MYTHS & FAQs*

Top Tips

INTRODUCTION

PREFACE

A friend, who never hitherto had reason to worry about her hair, came to me in panic, just recently. Her symptoms were not uncommon. Every time she used a comb, her hair came out in clumps. There were tell-tale strands all over her pillow, her clothes, the bathroom sink and tub. When she touched her head, she could feel right through its thinning 'cover' to the scalp.

Although she saw the primary problem as hair loss and blanched at the thought of going *ganja* (bald), her hair loss was only a manifestation of an underlying health problem, which I quickly diagnosed, and confirmed through tests and treated. Once the underlying problem was resolved, her hair loss also disappeared.

That hair should be such an accurate health barometer is, to me, just one of the many reasons that makes its study so fascinating.

That its health should be so vital to our physical appearance and psychological well-being is also what makes its study so crucial.

There is no denying the credo that the study of hair is a serious scientific pursuit. It should not be confused with the faddish prescriptions of fashion 'pundits' or hairdressers, posing as hair doctors. Solutions for hair problems are not to be found in fancy gadgets or potions 'dished-out' at 'amateur' parlours.

The business of hair care should rightfully be left to experts. Unfortunately, it has bloated into a multi-billion dollar industry invaded by big pharma and cosmetic companies with a host of self-grooming and style products that, in most cases, do more harm than good. With a motley crew of self-styled hair gurus, remedies are often worse than the hair disorders they claim to cure.

The specialised study of hair health is known as trichology. I am a trichologist, a medical doctor who specialises in diagnosing and treating conditions affecting the hair and scalp, including hair loss. I qualified at The Trichological Society, UK — the most prestigious professional organisation in the field — becoming its first-ever Indian graduate. I am honoured to be recently elected as its President — the first-ever Asian, in fact, the first non-UK citizen, to hold the post. This unique distinction has come my way in recognition of my efforts to integrate professional trichology with corporatised homeopathy, beginning with India.

What I hope to achieve with this book is a greater understanding that hair care is a medical, not cosmetic concern and needs to be addressed accordingly — an approach that may come to many as a breath of fresh hair.

Now, to the basics.

From time immemorial, hair has remained a prime physical attribute. Its colour, curl, condition, length and strength have long been the subject of fantasy, fable and fairytale. Samson derived his strength from his hair; Rapunzel's tresses roped in Prince Charming.

Healthy hair amplifies good looks. It adds to an attractive, youthful and desirable persona. It enhances your interaction with the world in terms of romantic as well as business relationships. It is a powerful sexual turn-on.

This is why loss of hair often leads to a visible, or noticeable, loss of confidence. One begins to feel unattractive and becomes self-conscious.

Besides imparting beauty, hair serves as an important diagnostic tool. Long lustrous locks indicate wellness whereas a dull, brittle mop may mean a lurking health problem.

Hair loss, for instance, may foretell the onset of diabetes much before it shows up in a blood test!

A study published at Harvard Medical School, US, found that, in men, hair loss concentrated on the crown (vertex; top) of the head, rather than the front, was linked with a three-fold greater risk of heart disease.

Drug abuse as well as toxicity can also be detected with a simple hair test, which has, in fact, been regularly employed as a medico-legal tool to solve legal, forensic and criminal cases.

Hair obviously has more to it than just cosmetic value. It is a living, luscious proof of your quality of life (QoL).

WHY HAIR INTERESTS ME & WHY IT SHOULD INTEREST YOU...

Hair is like a soaring flame; an object of desire.

It's probable that because it does not decay after death, the ancient Greeks and Romans believed that life resides in hair. In both Eastern and Western mythology, divine beings bear handsome heads full of hair. 'Thickly-maned' gods represent eternal youth, free from the ravages of illness and old age. Hair connotes youth, vitality, power and charisma. This is reason why the enticing goddess Hathor is called 'the lovely haired one,' while in *The Book of the Dead* seduction is represented as a bird-trap coiled from the beautiful hair of a woman.

In the *Bible*, while blessing the mother of Samson with a mighty son, God proclaims, "The razor blade will never pass over his head because he will be dedicated to God." Samson's colossal strength resided in his hair.

Legend has it that the enigmatic Cleopatra's glossy mane also came through divine blessing and, thereafter, was devotedly tended with oils and mystic potions.

Not much has changed since then. Women continue to lavish attention upon their hair. Nothing affects the psyche of a woman, or better mirrors her mood like the state of her hair. Bad hair days are not an invention of comedy writers; they really do exist. And you cannot help but endear yourself to any member of the fair sex by professing amazement at either her stunning new figure, or hairstyle!

Men are equally vain. From heads of states and politicians, cinema and sports idols to regular folk, hair is a crucial part of self-image. A study reveals that the greater their hair loss, the less satisfied men were with their appearance.

The overriding concern with hair loss is 'appearing' older than one's age. Although more pronounced among younger men, the concern is common across all age-groups. Most men with hair loss claim they don't care about hair loss. But this is not so. An actor who has played James Bond is supposed to have said, "I don't understand men who want hair transplants." Perhaps, a classic case of protesting too much since he himself conceals his baldness with a wig! In actual fact, men remain deeply worried about hair loss and are constantly on the look out for ways to 'reverse' it.

Hair treatments and transplants are certainly more common among men than women. However, women are more traumatised by hair loss.

A study published in *The Journal of the American Academy of Dermatology*, comparing the psychological and psychosocial impact of hair loss among men and women, found that women

HAIR-FILE

- Hair loss can 'hijack' one's career

- Research suggests that people with hair loss don't quite get their promotions on time; what's more, some are even denied jobs

- People with a scalp full of hair feel more confident than people with a receding hair line

- Hair loss 'hurts' one's pride

- Anxiety and depression are strongly linked with hair loss

- Many men have seen their girlfriends walk out, 'thanks' to their bald pate

- Divorce rates are higher in couples, where the man is losing hair, or going bald

- There are reports in India where men, who have veiled their baldness, with a wig or hair piece, before marriage, have had to 'face the music' — divorce after marriage.

HAIR-FILE

- Hair is the fastest growing tissue in the body; second only to bone marrow

- On the average adult scalp, 35 metre of hair fibre is produced everyday

- More than 50 per cent of your scalp hair must be lost before baldness becomes apparent to anyone

- Split ends cannot be repaired; they need to be cut

- Each strand of hair can carry a weight of 100 gm

- Female hair grows slower compared to male hair

- Brushing is more damaging for hair than combing

- Hair grows faster in warm weather and slower during winters

- Elderly people have slower hair growth

- Hair grows more slowly at night than daytime

- When viewed in cross section, straight hair appears round, whereas curly hair looks flat

- A baby's hair begins to grow around the third month after conception

- The total number of hair follicles is determined before the baby is born and will never increase; it will only decrease over time

- Palms and soles, also lips are the only areas of the body that do not have hair.

with hair loss developed a more negative body image than men and were less able to cope with it. All research confirms that women are far more worried about the way they look. Hair loss causes them to feel insecure about their appearance and whether the world and the people around them will accept them. The same holds true for men, but to a lesser degree. Men with hair loss are often characterised by a withdrawn manner. They suffer from low self-belief and experience difficulty in taking decisions.

Lack of hair is not just considered unattractive and old-looking, it is actually a sign of penance, renunciation and grief. Monks, across religious beliefs, shave their heads as a symbol of moving beyond material and sexual existence. In India, men also shave their heads to denote a period of mourning for the loss of a loved one.

Here's a quick checklist on why hair health matters:

- Healthy hair denotes confidence, whereas hair loss is associated with an inferiority complex, low self-esteem, depression and even suicidal tendencies

- A German study showed that 41 per cent of men with full heads of hair were selected for job interviews as compared to only 27 per cent of balding men

- 50 per cent of men suffer from some degree of male pattern baldness, by age fifty

- Nearly 20 million women have significant hair loss at some point in their lives

- Millions of men and women take prescription medications to prevent or decrease hair loss

- Approximately 100,000 men undergo hair transplants every year.

Hair disorders have a significant medical connect. They can be pointers for any or all of the following conditions:

- Diabetes

- Heart disease

- Ovarian cysts, or polycystic ovarian syndrome (PCOS)

- Hypothyroidism

- Hyperthyroidism

- Autoimmune diseases (e.g., systemic lupus

erythematosus, or SLE, which affects the skin, joints, kidneys, brain and other organs)

⬛ Stress.

The psychosocial fallout of hair loss can include:

- Anxiety and depression

- Sexual dissatisfaction

- Troubled sleep, or sleeplessness; difficulty in getting into the sleep mode, waking up between 2:00am and 4:00am and having trouble falling asleep again

- Aversion to physical activity and 'lowered' memory

- 'Abnormal' emotional responses.

Triggers of hair loss include:

- Bereavement, the loss of a loved one or pet

- Separation anxiety; moving house, hospitalisation of a loved one, divorce or break-up in a relationship; migration or relocation, nostalgia for hometown or surroundings

- Stress. Although individual responses to stress vary, the most predictable outcome is hair loss

- Social environment and childhood traumas have a pathological effect on hair loss.

Research reveals —

- 75 per cent of men feel less confident following the onset of hair loss especially while speaking or interacting with women

- Women with hair loss prefer to deny and disguise rather than treat it because of social stigma attached to the condition

- 60 per cent of all bald men are the butt of social jokes at some point or another

- 40 per cent of women with hair loss have marital problems. 63 per cent report of career-related problems

- Divorce can lead to severe hair loss in women

- Women, who have lost a partner through divorce, or death, are twice as likely to have thinning or loss of hair than those who are happily married or single

- Women prefer men with hair. Although a majority of them claimed baldness did not affect mate selection, when presented with digitally modified pictures of men with and without hair, women repeatedly chose the former as more sexually attractive.

The good news is that today there are a host of medical and

HAIR-FILE

- When hair is wet, it can increase its length by 30 per cent; it returns to normal length after it has dried

- Africans and Europeans are more prone to balding than Asians

- Even one centimetre of your hair can reveal a lot about your behaviour in the past month – what you ate, drank and the environments you encountered

- The thickness of each stand of your hair is determined by your genes

- A human hair is stronger than a copper wire of the same thickness

- Hair is as strong as a wire of iron! It rips only after applying a force of roughly 55 kg and that too only after it has stretched itself 70 per cent

- It's a myth that when you pluck a (white) hair, two will grow back to replace it

- People who sell their hair for making wigs out of it need at least 6 inches of hair to sell – that's more than one year's hair growth

- 'Rapunzel' rocked children's literature with her tower-length golden hair; the Rapunzel syndrome is an extremely rare intestinal condition — a result from eating hair (trichophagia)

- The average man will spend about five months of his life in shaving.

surgical options to combat, treat and correct hair loss. While the outcome can certainly appear miraculous, it is important to have realistic expectations — not be fooled by 'miracle' cures — and find safe, scientific solutions for lasting results.

Recovering your hair is a first step towards achieving optimal confidence and fulfilment.

WHAT YOUR HAIR CAN (FORE) TELL ABOUT YOUR HEALTH

Hair has more to it than what appears on the surface. It says a lot more about us than what the stars foretell, or the latest hair styles symbolise. In fact, the health of our hair and scalp can provide doctors with insightful cues about a host of 'latent' health disorders.

Our hair is not just 'dead' protein; it is a pointer to what is happening deep inside our body and mind.

In addition, our hair, like our psyche, responds to both physical and emotional stressors, including underlying health deviations, waiting to raise their 'ugly heads' — much before apparent clinical symptoms manifest.

DRY, LIMP, THIN HAIR

This may be a 'cursor' for hypothyroidism. In some cases, the 'tell-tale' sign is hair loss on the eyebrows, especially in the outer third of the eyebrow.

SCALY OR CRUSTY PATCHES ON THE SCALP

This indicates psoriasis, a common skin disorder. It occurs when the skin goes for a 'toss,' sending out flawed signals that accelerate the turnover and growth of skin cells. The detection of psoriasis can help us prevent and treat more serious conditions — especially psoriatic arthritis, or painful swelling of the joints with scaly, psoriatic distress.

OVERALL THINNING

It's customary to shed about 50-100 hairs a day. But, when hair appears to be coming out in 'clumps,' it's time for action. A job loss can cause such hair loss. Likewise, a bout of flu or fever, illnesses like jaundice, typhoid and malaria can cause hair loss. Most importantly, diabetes and hypertension can also cause such hair loss, much before they may be clinically diagnosed.

DRY, BRITTLE HAIR BREAKS EASILY

This may be a sign of iron-deficiency anaemia, which reportedly affects 60 per cent of Indian women.

HAIR LOSS IN SMALL, CIRCULAR PATCHES

This kind of hair loss can be a sign of autoimmune disorders, early-onset diabetes and thyroid disease.

GREY HAIR

This is no 'red signal' to be concerned that you are getting to 'look old' too early. It is a 'tell-tale' sign of stress, depression, or emotional anguish. However, diffuse grey hair at a young age may be indicative of thyroid problems and vitamin B deficiency.

What does the 'loss' of hair behind hair loss connote? That it makes sense to consult a trichologist — a doctor who specialises in the science of hair and scalp — the moment you notice any change in your hair health and get your hair and scalp analysed. In other words, it only means that the health of your hair and scalp needs scrutiny and diagnosis — and, this is best done by a trichologist.

Even a routine check-up, when everything is 'normal,' would be imperative.

Because, prevention — along with early detection and appropriate treatment — is often better than cure.

THE HAIR STORY

You know me, don't you? I am your hair.

I am in your genes and genetically or biologically programmed to grow, right from the time you arrived in your mother's womb.

I continue to grow all though your life.

Like a child, I need to be loved and cared for. But unlike a child, pampering does not spoil me. In fact, I flourish and thrive on attention. The more you look after me, the better I grow.

When you neglect me and resort to quick-fixes to make me look better, because you are in a hurry, you impact my growth and endanger my life.

I may even stop growing; sometimes, permanently.

Your overdependence on chemical, often toxic hair products and cosmetic salon treatments, where I am coloured, dried, crimped, ironed, burnt, pulled, twisted and sprayed, is detrimental to my well-being.

In my interest, please stay away from —
- ☞ Choose a shampoo that has natural active ingredients that are safer for scalp than chemicals
- ☞ Untested and strong cosmetic products
- ☞ 'Hot' blow dryers close to the head
- ☞ Excessive exposure to the sun and wind
- ☞ Parlour treatments like perming, bleaching, highlights and hot oil treatments
- ☞ Poor nutrition. I am what you eat!

HAIR-FILE

Hair is more than just a cute 'wrap.' It performs a host of biological functions, apart from being a cover-up for most part of your body. It may also often grow in places you'd rather not want it to, especially if you are bald!

1. Hair protects your head

2. It keeps you warm in winter and cool in summer

3. It protects against sunburn

4. Eyelashes and nasal hair prevent dust and foreign particles from entering your eyes and nose

5. Hair has nerve endings — which give you that 'feel-good' factor after a head massage.

I can last for all your life, provided I have the right conditions. Besides your physical health, I need your emotional well-being.

I cannot bear high levels of stress.

Like you, I too need to eat to survive. I absorb nutrition from the food you eat from the blood vessels located under your scalp or skin. I grow in three phases: anagen, catagen and telogen.

I grow about half-inch per month during the **anagen** (growing) phase, typically ranging from 3-7 years.

Following the anagen phase, I stop growing; in fact I start to rest. This is called the **catagen** (regression) phase. This lasts about 2-3 weeks.

After I've stopped resting, I move into the **telogen** (falling) phase. This lasts for about 3-4 months. During the telogen phase, I appear inactive and I also shed or fall. You will find strands of me on your pillow, bed, clothing, comb and brush, or simply going down the sink when you bathe or shampoo.

This is normal — 'ringing out the old and ringing in the new.'

At the end of the telogen phase, I once more enter the anagen phase and begin to grow back to normal size.

This is the pattern of my life.

I can be coarse or fine. The thickness on your head is relative to the thickness of my shaft. When I have a coarsely thick shaft, for example, I have more bulk and body than when I am thin and fine.

I come in three colours — black, brown and blonde. My colour is determined by the pigments (melanin) that I am endowed with. These pigments reflect certain wavelengths of visible light

There are two primary pigments in my strand. The dark-pigmented eumelanin is what imbues my brown or black shade. The higher its concentration, the darker I appear. The lower its concentration, the lighter I appear. Pheomelanin imparts

HAIR-FILE

Hair is composed primarily of 'dead' proteins — about 88 per cent. The proteins are of a hard fibrous type known as **keratin**.

Hair may be divided into two parts — the root and shaft. The **root** of the hair is in the skin (epidermis) of scalp. A pouch-like structure called **follicle** surrounds the hair root. The base of the hair root is in the shape of a **bulb**.

The **hair shaft** has three layers — the **cuticle, medulla** and **cortex**. Cuticle is the outer layer; it protects the inner layer. A healthy cuticle gives a shiny appearance to hair; unhealthy cuticle gives just the opposite effect. Medulla is the innermost layer, composed of large cells. Cortex is the layer between the cuticle and medulla; it 'houses' the 'colour-giving' melanin pigment and keratin. Cortex also determines the bulk and strength of hair.

The hair follicle contains sebum (oil). This gives lustre, or shine, to your hair.

the blonde or reddish colour. The size, amount and distribution of melanin in my body determines my colour. When I am bereft of melanin, I turn grey or white.

I am easy to understand and easy to look after. Treat me well and I will remain with you forever — as your crowning glory, or essential part of your good looks.

HEALTHY & UNHEALTHY HAIR

HEALTHY HAIR

- A healthy scalp has natural, healthy hair. A healthy scalp is porous — in other words, it has healthy pores. Each pore contains multiple hair shafts. This is why anyone with hair loss often presents with empty spots in the pores and on the scalp

- A soft texture denotes healthy hair

- Healthy hair can move easily, because the texture is soft

- As you may also know, healthy hair has adequate elasticity and tensile strength. This allows it to stretch and recover — without breaking

- Healthy hair has a natural sheen, or lustre — as the outermost layer of the hair shaft reflects light. It has elasticity; it can stretch more than just a little. It does not get tangled when wet. The water content of healthy hair gives it a straight feel or appearance.

Unhealthy hair, on the other hand, 'swells up' when exposed to water, air or humidity. It also becomes more curly, coarse and dull.

UNHEALTHY HAIR

- Is dry and rough. This may also be due to lack of proper hydration, or exposure to sun, chlorine and harsh chemicals

- Is limp, flat and lifeless

- Is brittle; breaks easily

- Has knots

- Is dry and rough with a 'straw-like' feel, especially towards the ends

✂— Has split ends

✂— Is vulnerable to dandruff.

Damage to the hair cuticle causes the hair to bulge and affects the lustre.

The following are the 'tell-tale' signs of damaged hair:

- Rough texture
- Lack of porosity or permeability
- Dry and brittle to touch and feel
- No elasticity
- Inclined to breakage
- Is spongy and matted when wet
- Colour fades too quickly; is prone to dandruff.

DRY, BRITTLE HAIR

Healthy hair, as you know, has a favourable permeability, or porosity. It also maintains moisture levels.

When the cuticle layer is raised from a healthy hair shaft, it allows the hair to absorb natural moisture.

When hair has defective porosity, usually as a result of over-processing, it results in damaged, dry and brittle hair.

HAIR LOSS TEST

We all lose hair, about 50-100 strands, everyday. Hair loss, which is more than 'normal,' disturbs us so much that we try all kinds of home remedies — to avoid seeing a doctor. What is critical is to know where to draw the line and head straight for a consultation with a professional trichologist.

The following test helps you to know whether or not your hair loss has become a cause for concern and needs medical attention.

 Tick your answers to the questions:

1. **Do you lose more than 50-60 hair strands a day?**

   ☐ Yes

   ☐ No

2. **Is your scalp visible in the area where you have lost hair?**

   ☐ Yes

   ☐ No

3. **Do you feel you now have less hair on your head than you had last year?**

   ☐ Yes

   ☐ No

4. **Has your hairline receded?**

   ☐ Yes

   ☐ No

5. Do you see a lot of your hair on the pillow, floor of your house, the bathroom sink or drain, in the comb etc.?

    ☐ Yes

    ☐ No

6. Is your hair less dense than before? Did you have thicker hair earlier?

    ☐ Yes

    ☐ No

7. Have you been experiencing hair or scalp problems for more than a few months?

    ☐ Yes

    ☐ No

8. Do you have a family history of hair loss (parents, siblings, paternal or maternal grandparents, uncles, or anyone in the immediate family)?

    ☐ Yes

    ☐ No

9. Do you suffer from any hormonal problems (thyroid disorders, ovarian cysts, irregular periods, menopause), or have you recently delivered?

    ☐ Yes

    ☐ No

10. Do you suffer from any scalp problems such as dandruff or greasy scalp?

    ☐ Yes

    ☐ No

11. Does your scalp itch ?

    ☐ Yes

    ☐ No

12. **Have you subjected your hair to chemical procedures, such as hair colouring, bleaching, perming and straightening?**

    ☐ Yes

    ☐ No

13. **Do you use hair products such as hair gels, mousse, hair sprays?**

    ☐ Yes

    ☐ No

14. **Does your hair/scalp problem affect your self-confidence?**

    ☐ Yes

    ☐ No

15. **Do you feel insecure about your appearance when you see someone with more healthy and beautiful hair?**

    ☐ Yes

    ☐ No

16. **Do you feel older than your age or less attractive due to your hair/scalp problems?**

    ☐ Yes

    ☐ No

Count the number of 'Yes' you ticked.

Your Hair Score [   ]

Your Test Results: If you answered **4 or more** questions with a 'Yes,' it is imperative for you to consult a trichologist for professional advice on your hair problems and suitable treatment.

Do not ignore your hair problems — they may reach a 'point-of-no-return,' sooner than you may think!

TYPES OF HAIR & SCALP PROBLEMS

MALE PATTERN HAIR LOSS

Male pattern baldness (MPB), or androgenetic alopecia (AGA), is one of the principal forms of hair loss (alopecia). It presents with not just depleting, or depleted, crowning glory on your scalp, but it can also trigger major emotional and psychosocial problems, especially in young men.

The disorder, as the name androgenetic alopecia suggests, has genetic 'roots' in 80 per cent of individuals. The mode of transmission is, of course, not just one, but from multiple genes (multigenetic).

The 'disorder' develops, gradually over 15-30 years. However, there is often a decline in hair thickness, or density, for several years preceding its advent, or actual manifestation. This is the best time to start appropriate and effective treatment to stall the slide.

Research suggests that the earlier the onset of male pattern hair loss, the greater the severity of the condition. Research also suggests that the existence of a strong family history on the mother's side is often weighed down by relatively poor treatment results. Also, as the name suggests, pattern baldness follows a distinct pattern.

MPB, in its early stages, affects the frontal area and the vertex (top, or crown) of the head. When it spreads over time, the occipital (back of the head) and the parietal areas (sides) remain, more or less, unaltered.

A **hair survey** of 4,000 respondents, conducted at **Dr Batra's,**

HAIR-FILE

Male pattern baldness affects 20 per cent of men at age 20. It affects 50 per cent of men, at age 50.

Statistics suggests that more than 90 per cent of hair loss consultations with a trichologist are related to male pattern hair loss.

A study reveals that 41 per cent of men with normal hair were selected for job interviews as against only 27 per cent of balding men.

Divorce rates in the UK, for instance, were found to be higher among balding men.

indicates the impact of hair loss —

53 per cent of men and 56 per cent of women, in the general population, think that men with hair loss look at least five years older than their actual age.

A whopping 79 per cent of men clearly reported that if they started balding, it would definitely affect their self esteem.

78 per cent of men and 75 per cent of women agreed that balding men were less attractive.

Tell-tale Signs

(Tick box below to do your own hair loss test)

If you have ticked **3 or more** of the following, you may most likely have male pattern baldness. Consult your trichologist.

☐ Family history of hair loss

☐ Hair strands 'decorate' your brush, or fall on your pillow, drain, sink and around your house

☐ A 'thinning' area on the crown (top) area of head

☐ Thinning of hair of the 'front portion' of your head

☐ Hair loss starts gradually or suddenly (Note: In times past, hair loss would start in one's thirties; today, even men in their twenties experience significant hair loss)

☐ Too slow or no hair re-growth

☐ Reduced hair thickness or density

☐ Receding hairline and longer duration between hair cuts. You go for a hair cut, because the hair on the sides seems to grow more than those on the top.

Your Hair Score [   ]

HAIR LINE TEST

What is Your Take? Check box:

☐ If your hairline touches the highest crease, your hair has not receded

☐ If your hairline is 1/3 to 2/3 inch away from the highest crease, your hair has started to recede

☐ If your hairline is more than 2/3 inch from the highest crease, your hair has definitely receded.

Baldness may progress, through different stages, as shown in the illustration below. It would help if you take a look at the illustration (below), highlighting male pattern baldness. Now — can you 'spot' the type of hair loss you have?

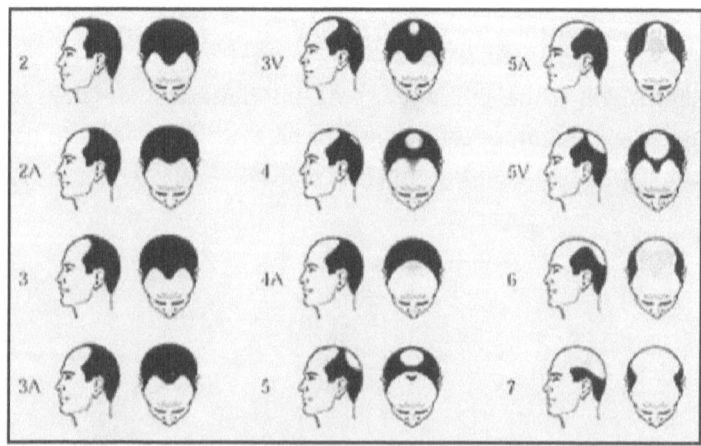

FIGURE I: HAMILTON-NORWOOD SCALE FOR HAIR LOSS IN MEN: RATE YOURSELF

KNOW YOUR TYPE

Stage 1:
No hair loss. The head is full of hair.

Stage 2:
Minor recession from the hairline, with some temporal (side of the head, or temple) recession. This stage is not called balding.

Stage 2A:
Recession progresses across the entire frontal hairline.

Stage 3:
Temporal recession deepens.

Stage 3A:
Frontal recession keeps progressing backwards.

Stage 3V:
Loss of hair in the frontal and temporal (side of the head) areas; early hair loss from the crown (top, or vertex).

Stage 4:
Frontal and temporal hair loss progresses; there is enlargement of the bald patch on the crown.

Stage 4A:
Hair loss progresses past the mid-crown.

Stage 5:
Bald area in the front enlarges and joins the bald area on the top of the head.

Stage 5A:
Bald patches in the front and at the top fuse and keep enlarging. The back part of the bald area is narrower as compared to Stage 6.

Stage 5V:
The bald patch on the top enlarges, although it has still not fused with the bald area at the front.

Stage 6:
Frontal bald area and on the top are fused and continue to enlarge. The back part of the bald area is larger than in Stage 5.

Stage 7:
Extensive baldness, where only a strip of hair remains at the back and sides of the head.

Causes

Hair growth cycle in men, with pattern baldness, produces shorter and thinner hair with each advancing cycle. This happens under the influence of the hormone, dihydrotestosterone (DHT).

In simple terms, what this means is that each time a man's hair falls out, new hair that comes up is thinner than the earlier strand — it also does not grow as long. It is lighter in colour as well.

In other words, male pattern baldness gets worse by a 'shade' every year. In the end, what is left is **very thin**, 'peach-fuzz,' or **fair hair**.

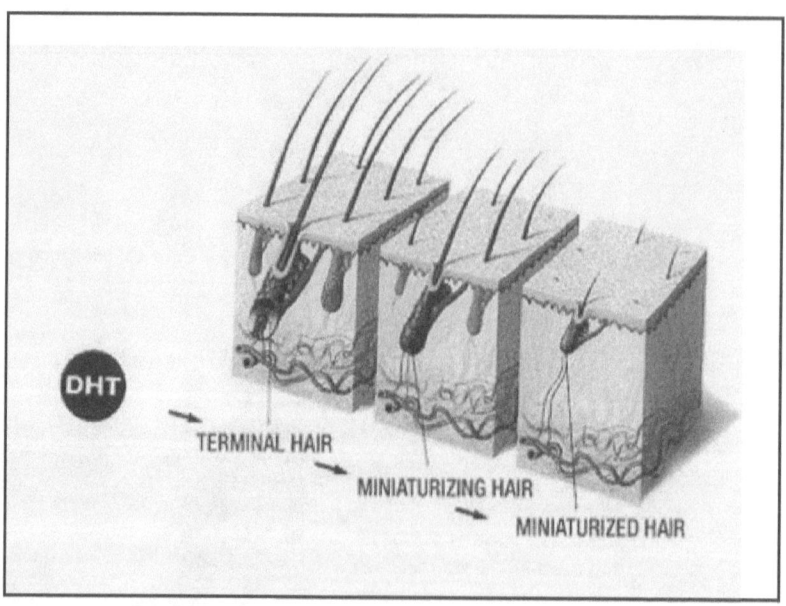

FIGURE 2: THE DHT-EFFECT

Now, you may well ask — is there any hope to stop a receding hair line in male pattern baldness? The answer is 'yes' and 'no.' YES, if you start treatment early, because you still have time to do something about it. NO, if you ignore, or allow the problem to get out of hand — because, you will soon reach a point, where you can do nothing about it.

LOST & FOUND

Look at the head of any balding man — you will, more often than not, notice that hair on the back and sides of the scalp are not affected by baldness — there may even be dense growth of hair in the area. This is the reason why many bald men actually fancy the thought of a haircut, sooner than later — thanks to the 'irony' of quick, intense hair growth in the area. This happens because the hair follicles on the side and the back of the head are not sensitive to the effects of DHT; this also actually prevents them from getting shrunk or 'miniaturised.' As a result, hair continues to grow normally and remains dense.

There is always an advantage with an obvious disadvantage — it is precisely this ability of hair strands, which grow all through life, that come in handy for hair transplantation.

THE BIG QUESTION

This brings us to a predictable query: "My dad is bald, so will I go bald too?"

No need to 'play' Nostradamus. A genetic test is all that may be required to confirm the presence of the 'balding' gene. However, the fact also is that if you have a family history of balding — maternal and paternal — or, you started losing hair at a young age, your hair loss will take a longer time to respond to treatment.

DHT & THE HAIR CONNECTION

Hair loss is primarily a result of excess male hormone (testosterone). Put simply, testosterone + 5-alpha reductase, an enzyme = dihydrotestosterone (DHT), a major cause of hair loss in both men and women.

It is important to have proper nutrition to maintain and nourish hair. Because, when DHT penetrates the hair follicles, it tends to prevent proteins, vitamins and minerals from providing the required nourishment to sustain 'life' in the hair follicles. The result is either a shortened growth phase or extended resting stage of the hair follicle.

DHT may also shrink the hair follicle — the hair follicle, therefore, gets smaller and finer. This is referred to as miniaturisation, because of which hair eventually falls off.

Research suggests that DHT may be implicated in 90 per cent cases of hair loss, because individuals who lose more hair — men or women — are more susceptible to the effects of DHT.

DHT reduces the growing phase and extends the resting phase of hair.

It has been clinically proved that two homeopathic remedies, *Thuja Occidentalis* and *Sabal Serrulata* — both natural DHT-blockers or inhibitors — have the therapeutic ability to block the synthesis of DHT, at the molecular level, and, thus, help to prevent and treat 'DHT-engineered' hair loss from the 'root.'

1. Include green tea and flaxseed in your diet plan. They are useful to 'elbow-out' the effect of DHT; they also help to prevent and control hair loss.

2. Speak to your trichologist for appropriate dosage of the two homeopathic remedies — if they are indicated for your type of hair loss.

This, however, does not mean that you give up hope, without exploring possible treatment options.

The best thing one can do is to diagnose hair loss problems, if any, early, and initiate suitable treatment, without losing time. Once this is done, you may have a good chance to slow down the progress of your hair loss, or balding.

Remember, a 'hairy' resolve, followed by appropriate treatment, is in your hands — not in your sun sign, or astrology chart.

DIAGNOSIS

A trichologist can easily identify male pattern baldness and 'stage it' appropriately with a video microscope.

Video microscopy is a painless, non-invasive technique. It magnifies hair follicles and the scalp up to 200 times. It helps to detect hair thinning early — before it is visible to the naked eye! Besides, it provides a microscopic view of the scalp and determines the status of your hair follicles. It can also help to measure and compare hair density, or thickness, in different areas and over a period of time. In the process, it can help to monitor and record the progression of treatment.

A susceptibility to hair loss can also be predicted with video microscopy — in other words, the technique can help analyse and foretell possible hair loss years before it actually occurs.

What does this imply? The earlier your hair loss is diagnosed, the better your success rate with suitable treatment.

HAIR-FILE

Hair follicles, which are most sensitive to DHT, are located in the front and top portion of the head. This area is most prone to hair loss.

In other words, when such genetically 'predisposed' hair is 'affected' by DHT, they tend to have a relatively short growth phase. So, instead of 4-6 years, the growth cycle reduces to 3-4 years and, thereafter, to 1-2 years. In due course, such hair follicles stop producing new hair, leading to baldness.

The horse-shoe shaped area covering the back and sides of the head has hair follicles that are not sensitive to the effects of DHT. Result: one never ever loses hair in this area.

There are other pointers that your trichologist will also look at —

 Pattern of your hair loss

Reduction in hair density, or thickness, accompanied by a 'loss' in hair diameter — each strand is thinner and straighter

Thick hair being replaced gradually by thin, or 'peach fuzz' hair

Increased dandruff (seborrhoeic dermatitis) of the scalp.

In addition, your trichologist may also order certain lab and other tests to confirm diagnosis or the likely cause of your hair loss.

RISK FACTORS

A variety of genetic and environmental factors are thought to play a role in the development of male pattern baldness.

Age. More than 50 per cent of men over the age of 50 have some degree of hair loss. Male pattern baldness in men can start as early as in their teens; the risk increases with age. In women, hair loss due to pattern baldness (androgenic alopecia) is most likely after menopause.

Male pattern baldness also follows a symmetrical pattern —

➤ 25 per cent hair loss may occur at age 25

➤ 40 per cent at age 40

➤ 50 per cent at age 50.

Family History. Male pattern baldness tends to cluster in families; having a close relative with pattern hair loss appears to be a likely risk factor for developing the condition.

Genetics. Sons always inherit the X chromosome from their mothers; when it comes to hair loss, they also seem to take after their fathers. Research shows that several genes inherited from both parents are to 'blame' for hair loss. The recently-found gene variant — as revealed on chromosome 20 — which is also said to be associated with male pattern baldness, supports the view.

TREATMENT

The basic aim of treatment is to slow down, control, or 'arrest' the progression of hair loss and try to facilitate hair growth.

Medical treatment works favourably in the early stages of hair loss — especially to slow down the progress of hair loss up to Stage 5.

Treatment may not, however, be the only solution for Stage 6 and

Stage 7. A 'camouflage' — i.e., wearing a wig, or undergoing hair transplantation could also be needed.

Stage	Treatment Options
1	Medical
2	Medical treatment/camouflage (e.g., hair fibre)
3	Medical treatment/camouflage/hair transplant
4	Medical/camouflage/hair transplant
5	Medical/wig/hair transplant
6	Medical/wig/hair transplant
7	Medical/wig/hair transplant

CASE ILLUSTRATION

Vipul, a business executive, came to our Clinic with hair loss. He said he'd lost almost 40 per cent of his scalp hair during the last three years.

His scalp showed balding areas on the crown. He said there was a strong family history on either parental side. His close relatives, especially his maternal uncle, had a clear predisposition for baldness before they had turned 35.

Vipul said there was no room for leisure, because of his high-pressure, stressful job. He said he had spent but little quality time with his family. He also reported that he often took refuge in smoking and alcohol to overcome his stress.

Worse still, he added, that his receding hairline was giving him a complex. He feared that this could affect his performance at work and also his annual appraisal.

Vipul's symptoms were typical of male pattern baldness (MPB), or androgenetic alopecia (AGA).

We prescribed him an appropriate homeopathic remedy and asked him to reduce and give up smoking and alcohol over time. After one year of treatment, we saw a healthy change in his hair loss — which was now under 'normal' limits.

For more patient testimonials, visit — http://www.youtube.com/drbatrasgroup

REALISTIC 'HAIR HOPE:' *WHAT TO EXPECT FROM TREATMENT*

What are my chances of re-growing my lost hair?

Pattern hair loss progresses by one grade each year. The idea should, therefore, be keyed to keep your hair from further decline. If timely treatment can achieve this prospect, it would be more than good.

If you want to give yourself a fuller look, there are certain 'camouflage' options that you'd give a try — such as wigs.

I have inherited pattern hair loss from my family. How come my brother isn't bald?

This is genetic. It can sometimes skip, a generation or two, before manifesting itself. A genetic test can suggest the trend, so as to promulgate appropriate treatment.

How come some people bald more than others?

This is again related to your genes. What you do about it is important — through early gene tests and treatment. Whether you will reach Grade 7 (in men) and Grade 4 (in women), the key, again, is to take suitable treatment, early — this may help 'arrest' hair loss.

How come hair on my body grows well, while hair on my head falls off?

The pool may be the right 'tool' to 'spot' hair loss. Have you ever seen men with hairy backs and shoulders, on the poolside, often showing a bald head or sporting a wig? You sure have. The poolside is an excellent place to observe such hair patterns. It shows that the gene for hair on the back and shoulders is different for hair on the scalp. DHT is 'ironically' nourishing for shoulder and back hair; what it also actually 'triggers' is a drop in head hair in several men.

➡ In typical male pattern baldness, natural DHT-inhibiting foods, such as soya are recommended

➡ Quit smoking and reduce alcohol intake. Smoking and alcohol are known triggers of pattern hair loss

➡ Avoid red meat, since it is believed to be a DHT-activator; it can worsen pattern hair loss

➡ Include green tea and roasted sesame seeds in your diet; they are natural DHT-inhibitors and help control hair loss

➡ 'Up' your protein intake. Proteins — e.g., milk and milk products, pulses, legumes, and soy — are good for hair

➡ Biotin, a vitamin, is evidenced to facilitate hair growth. Include rice bran, peanuts, soybean, cauliflower and mushrooms, which are rich in biotin, into your diet plan.

FEMALE PATTERN HAIR LOSS

Female pattern baldness (FPB), or androgenetic alopecia (AGA), is one of the most common forms of hair loss after male pattern hair loss.

It does not, in spite of its prevalence, catch the eye as much as male pattern baldness, because it does not quite progress to a state of complete baldness.

However, any which way you look at it, hair loss in women has as much impact on a woman's psyche as 'aging' itself.

A survey of 4,000 respondents, conducted at **Dr Batra's**, indicates that—

HAIR-FILE

About 10 per cent of women present with hair loss before menopause (cessation of menstrual periods). About 40 per cent show hair loss after menopause — between ages 50 and 60.

Hair loss has major psychosocial implications in women. It is often distressing and is accompanied by low self-esteem, a forlorn sense of being less attractive, along with nervous disquiet, or anxiety, in social circles.

- 79 per cent of women in the general population feel apprehensive about their appearance when they see someone with more healthy and beautiful hair.

- 80 per cent of women believe that men give preference to women with longer hair.

- 74 per cent of women responded saying that they were significantly worried about how society perceives them, if they were suffering from hair loss.

The inference is obvious — hair plays a vital role in a woman's life. A head full of lustrous locks for a woman exemplifies beauty, feminine grace, élan and poise.

Female pattern baldness can be classified on the following pattern (Figure 3).

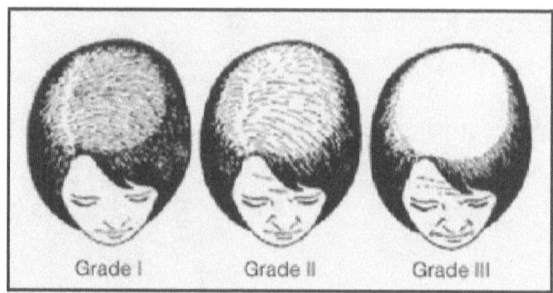

Grade I   Grade II   Grade III

FIGURE 3: LUDWIG PATTERN FOR HAIR LOSS IN WOMEN: RATE YOURSELF

A case in point. Women affected by hair loss may show hair thinning on the scalp when hair is parted in the midline. The exposed area resembles a 'Christmas tree.' A small percentage of women with hair loss may also 'show' male pattern baldness.

Tell-tale Signs

(Tick box to do your own hair loss test)

If you have ticked **3 or more** of the following, you may most likely have female pattern baldness. Consult your trichologist.

☐ Gradual hair loss with loss of density over time

☐ Hair strands 'adorn' your hair brush, or fall on the pillow, in the sink, or floor

☐ Scattered hair loss

☐ Hair strands appear thinner than before

☐ Hair looks less voluminous

☐ The plait, or ponytail, appears thinner, or the bun smaller than before

☐ Leaving the hair loose may not cover the gaps on the head

☐ 'Christmas tree' pattern — where the sides of the partition and the top portion of your head may show significant thinning (see Figure 4)

☐ Family history of hair loss.

Your Hair Score [   ]

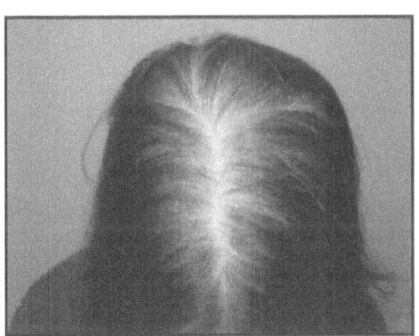

FIGURE 4: 'CHRISTMAS TREE PATTERN'

There is a distinctive relationship, in women, between their mother, sisters, aunts and grandmothers — when it comes to hair thinning patterns.

Unlike men, genetic hair loss in women affects the back of the head and also the sides.

Causes

Female pattern baldness (FPB), like male pattern baldness, is triggered by hormonal imbalance in the body. Conditions, such as ovarian cysts (or, PCOS), or menopause, are exclusive triggers for female pattern baldness.

What also activates the disorder is a fall below normal levels in the 'hair-protective' female hormone, oestrogen, in the body. This 'ups' the level of the male hormone, testosterone, in the body — the result is hair loss in women.

The 'saving grace' is, unlike men, DHT-sensitive hair follicles in women are spread diffusely all over the scalp. Hence, they don't 'go' bald like men (in front and top of the head), but lose hair diffusely all over the scalp.

The other basis of female pattern hair loss is genetics — the problem tends to run in families and is passed on from one generation to the other.

DIAGNOSIS

Your trichologist will evaluate the extent of your hair loss and its chronology, followed by certain lab and other tests.

For menopausal women, with female pattern baldness, there is no need for investigations, because the cause is obvious.

Similarly, a family history of baldness (on either side) is generally enough to decode whether the cause is genetic.

As far as ovarian cysts are concerned, your trichologist may examine you for abnormal hair growth on the body, excess facial hair and acne. Or, enquire if you have irregular periods.

Female pattern baldness is also usually diagnosed based on —

➤ The appearance and pattern of hair loss

➤ Other signs of too much male hormone (androgen), such as abnormal new hair growth on the face

➤ Changes in menstrual periods

➤ Blood tests may be used to diagnose disorders that cause hair loss

➤ Ultrasonography (USG).

TREATMENT

Treatment is aimed at slowing down the progress of hair loss and facilitating growth of hair. In advanced cases, the individual may require to wear a wig or hairpiece, or undergo hair transplantation.

QUESTION TIME

Will my pattern hair loss respond to medical treatment?

FPB can affect females from their teenage years. It also occurs commonly after menopause. The hair loss process is not constant and usually occurs in fits and bursts. It is not uncommon to have accelerated phases of hair loss for 3-6 months, followed by periods of stability lasting 6-18 months. Without medication, FPB tends to progress in its severity.

The duration of therapy, of course, depends on the stage of hair loss and other factors, such as health of hair or scalp — this may take 2-3 months, or more, to respond to treatment.

This remains, more or less, identical for male pattern baldness.

➡ 'Up' your intake of natural DHT-inhibiting foods, such as soya

➡ Quit smoking and reduce alcohol intake — smoking and alcohol are known triggers of hair loss

➥ Avoid red meat, since it is believed to be a DHT-activator; it can worsen hair loss

➥ Include green tea and roasted sesame seeds in your diet; they are natural DHT-inhibitors and help to control hair loss

➥ 'Up' your protein intake. Proteins — milk and milk products, pulses, legumes, and soy — are good for healthy hair

➥ Biotin, a vitamin, is known to facilitate hair growth. Rice bran, peanuts, soybean, cauliflower, and mushrooms are rich in biotin. Include them in your diet.

HAIR LOSS IN PATCHES

Alopecia areata (AA) is one of the most common forms of patchy hair loss. It manifests as small, bald patches on the scalp. They may appear suddenly, or in a relatively short span of time.

Patchy hair loss is often noticed by the hairdresser, usually during a haircut. Sometimes, the patch may go unnoticed until spotted at the parlour.

Another interesting thing is the anatomy of patchy hair loss is not always predictable. The patch may remain as such for a long time or may quickly progress to involve large areas of the scalp — sometimes the whole scalp or even the whole body. This may, at times, happen in less than 15 days.

Patchy hair loss is not life-threatening, but it can cause significant damage to one's self-image. However, the good news is that this condition often responds well to treatment, especially during the early stages.

Most people affected by alopecia areata develop one or two small bald patches on their scalp. This persists for several months, following which there may be some re-growth, or no growth, in the affected areas.

Statistics suggests that approximately 2-3 per cent of the population, at some point in their lives, suffer from patchy hair loss. The condition in children is often intense and emotionally devastating — such children tend to isolate themselves, from family, friends and others, or appear withdrawn, shy and reserved (while their parents may show both alarm and angst).

Patchy hair loss is more than a cosmetic problem; it is a **medical problem**

When not treated suitably, or appropriately, it can progress to —

- Total loss of hair on the scalp (alopecia totalis)

- Complete loss of hair all over the body (alopecia universalis), including eyebrows, eyelashes and other parts of the body.

Tell-tale Signs

(Tick box to do your own hair loss test)

If you have ticked **1 or more** you may most likely have patchy hair loss. Consult your trichologist.

☐ One or more smooth, bald patches on the scalp

☐ Patches merge to form larger patches (There may be rapid hair loss in certain instances)

☐ Hair loss from the eyebrows, beard, moustache or anywhere in the body — this is, of course, rare

☐ Patches of baldness come and go on their own

☐ Some patches may fill up, while new ones appear

☐ Patchy hair loss after a period of stress.

Your Hair Score

Causes

Our body is intelligent. It has its own 'defence system.' For example, white blood cells (WBCs) — which act like a fortress defending us against bacterial and other infections. When white blood cells mistakenly attack the body's own cells — instead of foreign invaders, such as viruses and bacteria — this is termed as an autoimmune condition.

Alopecia areata is an autoimmune condition, in which WBCs attack and destroy our hair follicles. This causes the hair to rapidly fall out, resulting in the formation of bald patches. The exact reason why WBCs start behaving this way is not clearly understood, although one or more of the following may be implicated:

- Genetics — one-fifth of individuals with patchy hair loss may have a family history of hair loss

- Thyroid disorders — this is often present in almost 20 per cent of people

- Anaemia

- Stress.

Other causes include a family history of diabetes, asthma, arthritis, lupus, vitiligo (white patches), Addison's disease (a disorder of the adrenal glands), nutritional imbalance or deficiency.

DIAGNOSIS

It is imperative for one to consult a trichologist to treat autoimmune conditions, such as patchy hair loss. A careful review of your medical history and blood tests should help your trichologist to recognise and treat the disorder.

Put simply, diagnosing alopecia areata is probably one of the easiest things for your trichologist, since the appearance of a bald patch is so apparent and distinct.

HAIR-FILE

50 per cent of patients develop alopecia areata before age 20.

34–50 per cent of patients with patchy hair loss recover within one year, although a majority may experience more than one episode of the disorder.

14–25 per cent of cases progress to total loss of scalp hair.

STRESS TO DESTRESS

Stress and hair loss need not be permanent. When you get your stress under control, your hair may grow back.

Talk to your trichologist if you notice sudden or patchy hair loss or more than usual hair loss when combing or washing your hair.

Sudden hair loss can signal an underlying stress or medical condition that requires treatment. If your attempts to manage your stress on your own don't work, speak to your trichologist about stress management techniques.

Blood, lab and other investigations — besides video microscopy to differentiate the type of hair loss — are often recommended.

TREATMENT

Patchy hair loss is technically 100 per cent curable, since there is zero-damage to the hair follicle.

Steroids. Steroids reduce inflammation. However, in patients with AA, steroids are used to stop the body's immune cells from destroying hair follicles. Steroids may be directly injected by your doctor into your bald patches or a topical steroid cream may be prescribed for application on the bald patches at home. Oral steroids are prescribed in extensive hair loss. Steroids seem to be okay for short-term use, but they are replete with side-effects on long-term use — such as osteoporosis, delicate skin and diabetes. Relapse rates are also very high.

Minoxidil. This is applied directly to the bald patches. Minoxidil is used to treat pattern baldness, but it also sometimes helps individuals having AA.

Cyclosporine. This potent immunosuppressant is most often given orally. Many doctors are reluctant to use it, because it can lead to high blood pressure and kidney damage, while suppressing your immune system.

DNCB. This is a chemical — dinitro chloro benzene. It has, in certain cases, 'caused' hair re-growth. It should, however, be taken only under strict medical supervision.

The most common treatment of alopecia areata is local steroid injections with/without oral steroids. However, studies conducted at **Dr Batra's** have shown that the relapse rate of patchy hair loss after steroids — not to speak of side-effects — is as high as 50 per cent, as compared to a rate of just 9.1 per cent after **homeopathic treatment.** It is also imperative for triggers, such as thyroid disorders, to be controlled for tangible results to emerge.

Medical treatment is often affordable. More than anything else, it is value for money, with good returns, and is well worth a try.

When hair begins to grow back in the bald patch, it is light in colour and thin initially. Over a period of time, the thickness gets better, just as normal colour is regained.

When patchy hair loss presents with large patches, or does not respond to treatment, the individual may resort to wearing a wig or hairpiece.

The duration of treatment will depend on the cause as well as the severity of the condition. Large and multiple patches obviously take a long time to be treated as compared to smaller and fewer patches.

Remember!

I have, in my experience, witnessed anxiety writ large on many an individual's face, teeming with questions, such as — "Will my hair loss spread to family members by way of touch, contact, sharing a comb, shampoo or hair brush?" The answer is a resounding NO.

QUESTION TIME

Will my hair grow back?

There is every chance — in fact, 100 per cent chance — that your hair will re-grow , more so, with timely treatment. However, it may also fall out again. No one can predict outcomes of hair re-growth in patchy hair loss, because the course of the disorder varies from person to person. Some people develop just a few bald patches — their hair re-grows and the condition seldom recurs. A few may lose all the hair on the scalp, face and also body. Yet, even in people who lose all their hair, the possibility for full re-growth remains a bright prospect. In some people, the initial hair re-growth, with medical treatment, is white — along with a slow return of their original hair colour. In others, however, the re-grown hair bears the same colour and consistency as the original hair.

➡ Increase your intake of proteins (soy, oily fish, eggs, chicken), beans and legumes

➡ Add whole grains, fruits, dark green vegetables, such as spinach, fenugreek, broccoli, cabbage and raw unprocessed nuts to your regular diet

➡ Include pumpkin seeds and flaxseeds — they nourish your hair from its roots

➡ Keep yourself well-hydrated; drink 2-3 litres of water daily

➡ Avoid or reduce your intake of tea, coffee and alcohol

➡ Avoid smoking, better still, give up smoking. Alcohol and smoking are bad for your hair health; they also lead to hair loss

➡ Reduce your stress levels with relaxation techniques, such as yoga or meditation.

SCARRING HAIR LOSS

Many skin conditions can lead to scarring. When the skin gets scarred, hair follicles in the skin are replaced by scar tissue — permanently. This is known as scarring hair loss or cicatricial alopecia.

Hair loss over such area is permanent and irreversible. No treatment can 'nurse' these hair follicles to grow.

Scarring hair loss can affect both men and women and people across all ages. In some cases, it forms slowly; in other instances, it may appear instantaneously, following a scalp injury.

Tell-tale Signs

(Tick box to do your own hair loss test)

If you have ticked **2 or more** of the following, you may most likely have scarring hair loss. Consult your trichologist.

HAIR-FILE

Some styling and grooming practices, at the parlour, such as hair rebonding, colouring, straightening or perming, can lead to scarring hair loss.

The reason being the inflammatory process and permanent scarring of the scalp can damage hair follicles, in some people, to the point of their demise.

So, there it is — if you fancy chemical or heated styling and grooming, at the parlour, you need to be aware of this possibility.

In the UK, trichologists are called as expert witness to dispose in such cases, especially law suits, against hair dressers for 'causing' hair loss.

Remember, the safest thing to do is to get a 'patch skin test' done, before using any product on your scalp or hair. This is especially appropriate for hair dyes and other chemical treatments.

☐ Hair loss, after parlour and other cosmetic procedures

☐ Hair loss, after scalp injury or damage

☐ Itching, burning, pain and tenderness of the scalp before a bald patch appears

☐ Redness in the affected area; there may also be pustules

☐ Skin loses its texture and shine in the affected area

☐ Skin in affected area may be hard to touch, or may be discoloured.

Your Hair Score [   ]

Causes

The condition typically occurs when the hair follicle is destroyed and is replaced with scar tissue.

Put simply, just about any injury, or infection, of the scalp can lead to a scar and cause scarring hair loss. In like manner, scarring hair loss can be triggered by the use of chemical relaxers, perms and hair colour that contains bleach.

Some skin conditions that can trigger scarring hair loss are as follows —

🔩 Lichen planopilaris. This condition is marked by purplish, raised, itchy, flat-topped lesions that heal with a scar

🔩 DLE (discoid lupus erythematosus). This is marked by irregular patches of hyperpigmented (dark) and hypopigmented (pale; white) skin, along with redness, scales, scarring and hair follicles devoid of hair

🐜 Kerion. Raised, spongy lesions on the scalp with pus discharge — these are formed in response to a fungal infection of the hair follicle.

Scarring alopecia may also result as a 'secondary' response to any of the following —

🐜 Acne (pimples) is not just the prime distressing 'preserve' of your face. A variant of acne can affect your scalp. This is more common on the back of the scalp

🐜 Injury to the scalp

🐜 Parlour burns — from hair dyes and chemicals used on the scalp, or severe local burns from heating instruments in the parlour. This is quite common; it is also easily avoidable.

DIAGNOSIS

Your trichologist will examine your scalp to check for any scarring. A 'hair pull test' may be performed to see how easily your hair gets uprooted in the affected area. In rare cases, a biopsy may be performed to confirm the diagnosis.

TREATMENT

Treatment outcomes are determined by the reduction, or disappearance of scalp symptoms such as itching, burning, pain or tenderness. Results are also evaluated by improvement in scalp inflammation, such as decreased redness, scaling or pustules, and by reduced hair loss.

Medical treatment cannot help one to regain hair in scarring alopecia.

QUESTION TIME

Will my hair ever grow back?

Hair will not re-grow once the follicle is destroyed. However, it may be possible to treat and/or control further deterioration.

It is, therefore, important to begin treatment as early as possible — to control the inflammatory process — although the progression of scarring hair loss is erratic. In some cases, progression is slow; in others, progression can be rapid and widespread.

Most often, there is sufficient hair remaining to cover the affected scalp areas. In certain instances, the hair loss may be extensive. This may call for the use of a wig.

➡ Avoid the use blow dryers and hair irons, or use them with extreme care; evade any kind of accidental contact with the scalp

➡ Counselling may be required in certain cases — for recognition and acceptance of permanent hair loss and wig use

➡ Do a patch test, before using hair products. Apply a small quantity of the product on a small patch of your skin, preferably behind ears, or nape of neck, or inner side of the elbow. Wait for 15 minutes and then wash off. Watch for signs of inflammation or allergy, such as redness, itching or rash

➡ Consult a trichologist immediately, if you notice any 'tell-tale' sign or symptom of scarring hair loss.

GREYING OF HAIR

Hair going grey, silver, or white is a natural part of aging.

Each hair is made up of two parts — a shaft, the coloured part, and root, the bottom part, which keeps hair attached to the scalp. The root of each strand of hair is surrounded by the hair follicle. Each hair follicle contains a certain number of pigment (melanin) cells. They give the growing hair shaft its colour — black, brown or blonde.

AGE

When we get older, the pigment cells in our hair follicles slowly wither. This leads to fewer pigment cells in the hair follicle. The result — hair strands no longer contain as much melanin as before. The hair now wears a more transparent colour — like grey, silver or white — as it grows. Eventually, the hair will look completely grey.

People can get grey hair at any age. Some people 'go' grey at a very young age, even in their teens, whereas others may go 'grey-haired' in their 30s and 40s. In some instances, it may take more than 10-12 years for all of a person's hair to 'go' grey. Greying spreads in the following sequel — the sideburns, beard, chest and the scalp.

How early one gets affected with grey hair is determined by your genes. This is one of the reasons why most of us start having grey hair around the same age that our parents or grandparents first did.

DIET

Lack of vitamin B12 (cobalamin) and folic acid can trigger grey hair, besides anaemia.

In a new study, researchers from Sweden report that when

participants suffering from vitiligo (white patches) increased their consumption of vitamin B12 and folic acid, through their diets and oral supplements, there was re-pigmentation of grey hair in 64 per cent of the patients, with six individuals experiencing total re-pigmentation.

SMOKING

Smoking can cause your hair to prematurely grey. A study in the UK found that smokers were up to four times more likely to have grey hair than their non-smoking counterparts.

DENTAL WHITENING PRODUCTS

The 'whitener' smile of your teeth-whitening toothpaste is also said to blot your hair colour. A study has shown that even a tiny dose of hydrogen peroxide, found in teeth-whiteners, can 'initiate' melanocyte 'death' — a likely trigger for colour change in your hair.

POLLUTION

Pollutants, chemicals, ultraviolet (UV) light and free radicals — by-products of chemical processes, responsible for aging and tissue damage — can impinge on melanin production, while impacting your hair's natural pigmentation, triggering grey hair.

GENETICS

Research shows that our genetics is behind greying hair. Our inheritance determines not only our hair colour, but also when hair greying begins.

HAIR CARE PRODUCTS

Strong chemical hair bleaches, dyes, conditioners and shampoos can contribute to greying of hair — sooner than later.

THYROID

Thyroid disorders can lead to grey hair, or diffuse grey hair at young age.

VITILIGO

This is a condition in which hair loses pigmentation in patches due to a decrease in melanin production. As a result, the hair follicles that grow after melanin loss have no colour — hence, the grey appearance, only in those patches affected by vitiligo.

STRESS

Emotional stress prompts a 'bad' chemical rush in our body, leading to melanin 'demise.' Result: grey hair.

Work or personal stress — or, more precisely, cellular stress — can also, likewise, turn your hair grey.

TREATMENT

Grey hair, caused as a result of conditions such as thyroid disorders, vitamin B12 deficiency and vitiligo in younger individuals can be treated effectively with appropriate homeopathic treatment. Speak to your trichologist, if you have such concerns.

EXCESSIVE HAIR (HIRSUTISM)

Nothing can be more disconcerting for a woman affected, by a quirk of hormonal 'glitch,' with excess hair — other than on her scalp.

The disorder is called hirsutism. It is characterised by excess facial and body hair.

Such hair is dark and coarse, because the abnormal hair growth usually occurs in places where men typically grow hair — chest, face and back.

Some women who face the unpleasant, distressing prospect of unwanted hair, turn to parlour treatments, such as threading and waxing, lasers and epilatory creams.

Tell-tale Signs

(Tick box to do your own test)

If you have ticked **2 or more** of the following, you may most likely have hirsutism. Consult your trichologist.

- ☐ Excess facial hair in women — on the chin (beard), upper lip, side-burns. Such hair is coarse

- ☐ Abnormal hair growth on the chest, around nipples, abdomen and back

- ☐ Irregular menstrual periods

- ☐ Acne (pimples)

- ☐ Loss of feminine body shape.

Your Hair Score

Causes

➤ Ovarian cysts or polycystic ovarian syndrome (PCOS)

➤ Tumours of the adrenal glands or ovaries

➤ Cushing's syndrome

➤ Certain conventional medications used for hair growth —
minoxidil; cyclosporine

➤ Danazol, used to treat endometriosis — a medical condition
in which the cells from the lining of the uterus (endometrium)
appear and flourish outside of the uterine cavity

➤ Anabolic steroids.

HIRSUTISM & LASER INDUSTRY

The latest fad for getting rid of excess hair is laser treatment. The treatment is speedy, efficient and permanent. The fact is the entire 'bludgeoning' laser industry thrives on hirsutism. However, the hazard is: when laser is not done carefully, it can cause burns.

Many women coming to me for treatment for hair loss report of having had a laser procedure to get rid of their unwanted body/facial hair. After detailed analysis of their case and on advising them certain investigations, one in five of them are found to be suffering from ovarian cysts (or, PCOS). We treat the cause and their problem gets resolved over a period of time. In my view, any case of excessive hair should not be ignored and must not be dealt with 'quick-fixes;' it is always important to treat the problem from the 'root.'

At times, some women with hirsutism may have normal levels of male hormones.

When no underlying cause, or trigger, is found, the cause of hirsutism may be difficult to ascertain.

There are also certain factors that may increase one's risk of hirsutism — they are genetics, race and ethnicity. Women having South Asian, Middle East and European ancestry are prone to develop hirsutism.

DIAGNOSIS

Diagnosis is often based on medical and family history, menstrual cycles and certain conventional medications taken. Your trichologist will examine for excessive hair growth and perform USG to check for tumours, or cysts, in the ovaries.

In addition, one of the following tests is ordered:

- Blood tests, which may show high androgen levels

- CT scan, MRI and pelvic ultrasound are used to find cysts (or, tumours) in the ovaries or adrenal glands.

➡ Many over-the counter (OTC) epilatory creams are available in the market to get rid of excess hair. Use with care

➡ Plucking/threading the hair (especially for facial growth), or waxing the excess hair

➡ Shaving is another easy option, though it may have to be done frequently

➡ Electrolysis — this is a permanent way to get rid of unwanted hair. It uses electric current to 'kill' each hair follicle one by one. It goes without saying that this is not feasible for larger areas.

DANDRUFF

Most of us have heard of the word, dermis. The dermis is the tough layer of connective tissue which is about 2-3 mm thick and provides strength to the skin.

It contains sebaceous (oil) and sweat glands.

The sebaceous glands generate an oily substance. It creates a 'wad' of wax (sebum) to cover the opening of the growing hair follicle on the scalp. Sebum acts as a lubricant, giving hair its wax-like shine, or lustre.

From the functional perspective, the sebum protects the hair shaft. It is a carrier of odours (pheromones) involved in sexual and social attraction. This is also how a newborn child recognises the mother's odour.

Too much of a good thing is sometimes not good. Excess sebum leads to unpleasant cosmetic and aesthetic effects, as also specific disorders. One of them is greasy hair. Greasy hair not only looks dull and moist, its thick, flat masses make hair difficult to comb.

When hair is 'loaded' with sebum, it gets adhered and flattened on the scalp. The real issue is even after wiping or washing, the sebaceous 'veneer' is quickly restored on hair.

This condition is called **seborrhoea**, derived from the Greek, *rheos,* meaning river. Most individuals having seborrhoea present with a greasy scalp and a greasy forehead.

Seborrhoea can have the following effects —

- Dandruff — a cause of hair loss on the scalp
- Darkened hair
- Dull, lustreless hair

- Moist, greasy look — adolescent hair has more sebum

- Stickiness; stuck hair

- Limp, flattened, non-curly hair

- Disorderly locks

- Hair is difficult to comb

- Hairstyles don't remain in place for long

- Itching of the scalp.

Dandruff is a scaly disorder of the scalp. It is extremely common, yet comparatively harmless, except for its role in hair loss and acne (pimples).

In adolescents and adults, the disorder is called 'dandruff.' In babies, dandruff is called 'cradle cap.'

Dandruff affects 40 per cent of the human population, worldwide.

Dandruff may not be a disease *per se*. It is also not life-threatening, or the basis for extreme anguish, yet the itchy white, scaly flakes that it presents with are not only annoying, but also emotionally distressing.

Tell-tale Signs

(Tick box below to do your own test)

If you have ticked **1 or more** of the following, you may most likely have dandruff. Consult your trichologist.

- ☐ Greasy, scaly and white (or, yellow) flakes that fall from the scalp

☐ Itching, redness and oozing of the scalp

☐ You find white flakes on your shirt, or clothing.

Your Hair Score ☐

Dandruff affects the hair bulb and its cycle. Researchers suggest that dandruff in all probability changes the hair cycle.

DARE TO WEAR BLACK!

Dandruff has damaging effects on one's emotions, social life and personal attractiveness, or how others perceive them. One also — man or woman — feels less attracted to someone of the opposite sex with dandruff.

Dandruff also affects the way a person dresses up — often avoiding black or darker clothes to keep the unsightly flakes out of view. It is this emotional aspect that the anti-dandruff shampoo industry banks upon heavily — urging you to try out their 'effective' shampoos and 'dare to wear black.'

Dandruff affects self-confidence and state of mind, no less. People are often anxious about having dandruff at important events — job interview, courting or marriage, party or during a presentation on the job.

Self Help!

➡ Keep the scalp clean by washing regularly. Use a natural dandruff cleansing shampoo, enriched with the homeopathic *Thuja Occidentalis* (white cedar), with clinically proven anti-dandruff properties, every alternate day. It is safe and effective

➡ Protect your hair from bright sunlight and pollution — keep hair covered while travelling

➡ Consume 2 tbsp of roasted powdered flaxseeds, everyday. Eat a serving of the probiotic yogurt (*dahi*) daily, for a healthy scalp

➥ In sticky dandruff, rinse scalp with sour milk or a mild solution of lemon juice (2 tbsp of lemon juice to 0.5 litre boiled cooled water)

➥ Dab the homeopathic *Calendula* cream to itchy areas around hairline. If whole scalp itches, apply flaxseed oil overnight. Sleep on an old pillow, or cloth, and rinse in the morning

➥ In severe dandruff, wash hair with a shampoo containing selenium

➥ Practice relaxation techniques, such as yoga or meditation, to ease stress.

PSORIASIS OF SCALP

Psoriasis is a common, genetically determined disorder of the skin and scalp. It consists of well-defined red plaques covered with a typical silvery scaling.

The course of psoriasis is erratic, changeable and chronic, with alternating relapses (worsening) and remissions (decline).

Tell-tale Signs

(Tick box below to do your own test)

If you have ticked **1 or more** of the following, you may most likely have scalp psoriasis. Consult your trichologist.

- ☐ Psoriatic patches on the back of the head (sometimes the whole scalp, or other parts of the scalp)

- ☐ Red patches of skin, covered with thick silvery-white scales (they may look like dandruff, at times)

- ☐ Severe itching (sometimes, it may not be itchy)

- ☐ Hair loss in severe cases

HAIR-FILE

According to clinical research studies conducted in the UK and Germany, 81-97 per cent of psoriatic patients treated with homeopathy showed distinct improvement, with no side-effects.

A study published in *The Journal of the European Academy of Dermatology and Venereology*, a conventional medical journal, reports that psoriasis patients experienced significant improvement in their quality of life (QoL) and reduction in their psoriasis symptoms with homeopathic treatment.

☐ White flakes on your clothes (similar to dandruff).

Your Hair Score ☐☐☐☐☐☐

Causes

Psoriasis is caused by your body 'overproducing' new skin cells. The condition affects both sexes, at any age, although it is somewhat uncommon in the first 2-3 years of life.

Certain circumstances, situations, events or states are known to ignite the initial attack and consequent recurrences — e.g., acute or chronic bacterial infections, stress and chronic alcoholism.

The precise cause of psoriasis is not known, although there are a host of factors that may possibly contribute to its development or progress.

While genetic factors may play a key role, studies suggests that about one-third of individuals who develop psoriasis may have one or more relatives with the disorder.

Some researchers blame psoriasis on a 'flawed' immune system, primarily because an increased number of white blood cells (WBC), 'soldiers of health,' are in attendance between abnormal layers of skin.

Other probable causes of psoriasis are:

➤ Temperature changes — cold, dry weather makes psoriatic symptoms worse

➤ Infections such as 'strep-throat'

➤ Stress, depression and anxiety

➤ Some conventional medications, such as non-steroidal anti-inflammatory drugs (NSAIDs; for example, nimesulide); diazepam (valium), a drug used for the short-term relief of symptoms related to anxiety disorders; and, anti-hypertensives (beta-blockers).

DIAGNOSIS

Scalp involvement may lead to hair loss and also reduction in hair density, or thickness. There is often **extensive hair loss** when psoriasis affects the entire scalp.

There are three types of hair loss (alopecia) in psoriasis:

✄ Hair loss confined to the lesions

✄ Acute 'telogen' hair loss — massive hair loss from all over the scalp in a short period of time

✄ Destruction of hair follicles giving rise to scarring hair loss.

The diagnosis of psoriasis is based primarily on its presentation, or appearance — the thick, red flaky patches, which are distinctive of the disorder. This isn't, however, as simple as the 'scales' sound, because even experienced doctors and clinicians find it difficult, at times, to diagnose psoriasis with certainty, because it can 'mimic' other skin disorders.

To confirm diagnosis, a skin biopsy or culture of skin patches is sent to the laboratory.

➡ Hair products containing shale oil are suitable for most individuals with scalp psoriasis

➡ Coconut oil is of particular importance in psoriasis of the scalp. A light scalp massage at night with some warm coconut oil helps to loosen the scales of psoriasis. The next morning gently wash off the oil with a mild, natural shampoo. The scales will come off, leaving you feeling a whole lot lighter! This will also help reduce itching of the scalp

- Cutting hair short helps control scalp psoriasis. The advantage is it makes treatment easy to apply, although it may not be 'pleasant' for everyone

- Phototherapy is effective, although difficult to deliver to the scalp. Special targeted devices and UVB combs have been devised for the purpose. They appear to be helpful. In certain cases, prolonged clearance has resulted from such a course of scalp and hair care

- Include flaxseeds in your daily diet — take 2 tbsp of roasted, powdered flaxseeds with water in the morning before breakfast and in the evening before dinner. This helps to control inflammation

- Avoid red meat. The inflammatory substance (arachidonic acid) in red meat is suggested to worsen psoriatic patches and inflammation.

HAIR LOSS IN CHILDREN

Hair loss, or alopecia, isn't just a problem for adults. It is responsible for an estimated 6-8 per cent of clinic visits for anxious parents worldwide.

Hair loss in children is a scary and frustrating prospect for parents, primarily because they don't expect their kids to lose hair. However, the good news is that, with proper diagnosis and professional treatment, most cases of hair loss in children can be managed successfully.

RINGWORM

Tinea capitis, or ringworm of the scalp, is a fungal infection. It is a common cause of hair loss in children.

It presents with scaly patches of hair loss on the scalp. The patches are generally round or oval. The hair may be broken off on the surface of the skin; they may also appear like black dots on the scalp.

Ringworm is contagious. Make sure your child does not share any objects that touch the head or scalp, such as towels, caps, scarf, pillow cases, or brushes.

A microscopic examination confirms the diagnosis.

PATCHY HAIR LOSS

Patchy hair loss, or alopecia areata, is characterised by the sudden appearance of round or oval patches of hair loss. The patches are glossy or smooth — there may be no scaling or broken hair.

It is reported that nearly 25 per cent of children with patchy hair loss may also have pitting and ridging of their finger nails.

Most children regain their lost hair within a year's time, albeit re-growth is erratic, or one may lose hair again.

About 5 per cent of children with the disorder may progress to alopecia totalis, or complete loss of all hair on the scalp. Some may also develop alopecia universalis, or total loss of body hair.

TELOGEN EFFLUVIUM

This type of hair loss emerges following a bout of high fever, flu or severe emotional stress. It occurs when hair in its growth phase is abruptly stunted and moved into its resting phase. The shedding, a 'mass migration' of hair follicles from growth into dormancy, can last for up to six weeks. The hair loss is not total; it may also not show up in patches. Hair typically appears thin throughout the scalp.

Most parents who visit their doctor are worried that their child may have a dangerous illness or disease.

The redeeming part is hair takes 3-6 months to re-enter the growth phase — although this makes hair restoration look like a slow, long drawn-out process.

TRACTION ALOPECIA

This is hair loss that occurs after physical damage to the hair. Traction alopecia is a common cause of hair loss, particularly in girls.

It can emerge due to fluffing, combing, washing, curling, blow drying, hot combing, straightening and bleaching.

A point to note here is the very hairstyles that are used for kids to make them look cute may be damaging to their hair.

Styles that apply tension to the hair, such as tight ponytails, braiding, barrettes and permanent weaving, can also damage the hair and trigger hair loss.

The hair will usually return, after counseling and treatment, but re-growth can be slow. Because, the 'injured' hair follicles do not heal quickly, they often take 3-6 months before they return to their growing phase.

TRICHOTILLOMANIA

This type of hair loss is caused when the child pulls, plucks, twists, or rubs his or her hair vigorously — owing to emotional distress, peer and parental pressure.

The hair loss is patchy and 'represented' by broken hair of varying length.

Patches are also most often seen on the side of the child's dominant hand.

Girls, having emotional problems, seem more inclined to pull their own hair, rather than boys.

Speak to a trichologist, if your child shows such symptoms — to evaluate emotional concerns and treat other underlying factors that 'trigger' hair loss in children.

HAIR LICE

Statistics suggests that hair lice, a common problem, affect millions of people worldwide.

Hair lice do not constitute a serious disease, yet they can cause a great deal of annoyance, embarrassment and itching 'frenzy' — especially in children.

The eggs of the adult female lice are called nits, which firmly attach to the base of the hair shaft. When the nit hatches into a baby 'louse,' called nymph, it grows into an adult louse in ten days and lives for about a month. Adult lice feed on blood; if they fall off from the head they die in just two days.

Tell-tale Signs

(Tick box to do your own test)

If you have ticked **1 or more** of the following, your child most likely has hair lice. Consult your trichologist.

☐   Itching of scalp

☐   Red sores, due to excessive scratching

☐   White dandruff-like appearance (This is because of lice eggs or nits that get attached to the scalp).

Your Hair Score [   ]

QUESTION TIME

Why are lice more common in children?

Sebum. Children produce much less sebum, or no sebum, in certain conditions — hence, they don't have the protective shield as adults do. They are, thus, 'open' to lice infestation.

Clustering and Playing. Lice are highly contagious. They can spread quickly from person-to-person, especially in group settings, such as schools, childcare centres, sports activities and camps. The most common route of lice transmission is head-to-head contact, such as two kids bending over the same toy, book, or electronic games.

DAMAGED HAIR

What is damaged hair? Damaged hair usually means hair cuticles (outer layer of the hair shaft) that are cracked, chipped, roughened or worn out. Such hair is characteristically rough to touch; it may also be dry and brittle. It is also easily prone to breakage.

Causes

Hair damage can be induced by a wide variety of things — chemicals, cosmetics, parlour procedures, when done incorrectly.

Tick what, among the following, may have caused damage to your hair — because any of these could cause hair loss

- ☐ Frequent bleaching or dyeing (chemical damage)
- ☐ Frequent perming, straightening, or curling the hair
- ☐ Washing the hair too frequently
- ☐ Vigorously rubbing the hair
- ☐ Use of dryers and other styling equipment frequently
- ☐ Use of inappropriate products and methods to style the hair
- ☐ Excess sun exposure
- ☐ Chemicals, toxic elements and pollutants in water
- ☐ Poor diet, or vitamin deficiency
- ☐ Stress

Your Hair Score ☐

Note: Any of the above can damage or weaken the hair shaft. The outcome is breakage and hair loss.

Hair growth usually resumes after the products/procedures are discontinued, unless the effects are excessively damaging and have caused immense harm to the scalp.

Speak to a trichologist, if you have any such concerns.

Damaging Hairstyles

Certain hair-styling techniques that pull tightly on the hair, for example, tight 'cornrow' braids and pigtails can lead to a type of hair loss called traction alopecia. Traction alopecia starts with hair loss in a marginal band, primarily in the front, sides and temporal areas. It may also be aggravated by headgear, wearing helmets for prolonged periods, pulling hair in bunches, tight plaits/pony tails, excessive handling of hair and amateurish massage treatment.

Split Ends

Splitting of ends is normally a problem of dry hair. It results in the tips of the hair being split or frayed.

Split Ends: Causes

Mechanical stress and excess heat are prime reasons why hair split. Vigorous brushing and use of chemical products, such as hair colours and relaxers may also cause your hair to split.

What to Do?

There is no real cure for split ends, though there may be creams that claim to 'repair' your split ends. The best way to get rid of spilt ends is to trim hair at regular intervals.

Problem of Vigorous Grooming

Too much shampooing, combing, or brushing far too many times can cause hair breakage. When hair breakage occurs, the hair appears dishevelled, or thin.

One should avoid fancy, or insensitive, embellishments on hair. It is also best to avoid rubbing wet hair vigorously with a towel to dry it, or comb. Rubbing vigorously can lead to hair breakage. This is because wet hair is more elastic and susceptible to breakage than dry hair.

➥ Steer clear of chemicals. If you must colour your hair, use ammonia-free colour

➥ Use a hair-friendly comb — avoid using hair brush. Avoid back-combing

➥ Condition your hair regularly; use leave-in hair serum

➥ Protect your hair — from harsh sunlight, in swimming pools (wear a swimming cap), damaging hair accessories and hairstyles

➥ Nurture well — eat a healthy diet, get plenty of water, sleep well and 'stress' less.

CAUSES OF HAIR LOSS

HORMONES AND HAIR

Hormones are body chemicals. They are essential for various bodily functions. They play a vital role in hair growth as well as hair loss. Hormonal balance is just as essential in the body as the ticking of your wristwatch. Hormonal imbalance not only upsets the body's working pattern; it also affects hair.

Hormones that relate to hair are testosterone, oestrogen and thyroid.

OESTROGEN

Oestrogen is primarily a female hormone, although it is also found in small quantities in men. It plays an important role in hair growth. It makes your hair growth phase last longer; it also improves the quality of hair.

The hormone is responsible for making a woman a woman, while distinguishing her from a man. Oestrogen not only imparts soft feminine features, it also gives that soft, petal-like gentleness to a woman's looks.

Have you ever wondered why a woman looks so beautiful during her pregnancy? Such glowing skin, lovely hair... It is because of this hormone. Although levels of this hormone rise and fall periodically each month, during pregnancy, it remains high for a long time. This results in longer, thicker, stronger and healthier-looking hair.

Ask any woman; she will agree that her hair always 'g(r)lows' best during pregnancy.

HAIR-FILE

Hairdressers often claim that they can figure out a regular client's pregnancy, even before the woman is ready to share the news with the world.

The lustrous mane, brought about by pregnancy, is a gift, thanks to liberal levels of oestrogen.

ORAL CONTRACEPTIVE PILLS

Oral contraceptive (OC) pills are artificial or additional source of oestrogen for the body. When the supply of 'artificial oestrogen' is stopped, the body reacts to sudden 'oestrogen withdrawal.' The result: testosterone is on the upsurge, resulting in excess hair loss. OC pills are a boon to the modern woman. They give women freedom of choice — for birth control and to regulate periods. It is, however, a bane when stopped.

TESTOSTERONE

Testosterone is predominantly a male hormone, although women also produce small quantities of it. The hormone separates the men from the boys, with typical growth of thick hair on the body — especially on the chest, abdomen, arms, legs and face.

At times, testosterone gets converted to DHT — when this happens it suppresses hair growth, where men want it the most — on their head. The result is male pattern baldness (MPB). This, in my experience, is the most common condition that trichologists treat at the clinic.

Testosterone effects normally remain subdued in women due to higher concentration of oestrogen. However, as oestrogen levels fall (such as after pregnancy, ovarian cysts or menopause), testosterone effects start to show — resulting in female pattern baldness.

Consult a trichologist to control hair loss.

THYROID & HAIR

The thyroid (pronounced *thy-royd*) is a gland. It is shaped like a little butterfly. It resides under the skin in front of your neck. To find it, just touch your throat in the Adam's apple area with one finger and the top of your breastbone — the flat bone that runs down the middle of your chest — with another finger. The thyroid gland is located in that small space in-between your fingers.

It moves up and down when you swallow. See if you can feel it — and, you will.

The thyroid gland produces special chemicals called hormones. The two major hormones that the thyroid makes and releases into the bloodstream are T3 (triiodothyronine) and T4 (thyroxine). All the cells in the body need thyroid hormones to work efficiently. Thyroid hormones manage how quickly the body uses up energy. They regulate our metabolism; they are also key factors in helping children grow.

The thyroid gland works like the thermostat in a gadget. If your thyroid gland is too active, it produces too much T3 and T4. It is like having a thermostat that's set too high; the gadget gets overheated. If it's not active enough, or if it's set too low, it, like the gadget, gets too 'cold.' Well, if it's making just the right amount of thyroid hormones, it keeps the temperature just right and balanced.

Research suggests that nearly half of all adults experience thinning of hair by age 40. Out of which about 20 per cent of individuals with thyroid disorders are evidenced to experience hair loss earlier and more quickly than the others.

Hair loss, therefore, tends to persist in thyroid patients, notwithstanding appropriate management and treatment.

Many patients also do not realise at all that their hair loss may be triggered by a thyroid disorder. They keep trying to manage their hair loss with different oils, shampoos, parlour therapies or even medication, but with no results. In fact, many of them come to our clinics complaining of nothing else but hair loss. However, when we suspect thyroid problems, based on their history and clinical signs, they are advised investigations, which confirm our suspicion in most cases — thyroid problem being the culprit.

 **Tell-tale Signs**

(Tick box to do your own test)

If you have ticked **2 or more** of the following, you may most likely have hyperthyroid-related hair loss. Consult your trichologist.

Hyperthyroidism (Too much thyroid hormone)

☐ Weight loss

☐ Heat intolerance

☐ Increased appetite

☐ Rapid heart beat

☐ Frequent stools

☐ Restlessness

☐ Anxiety/nervousness.

Your Test Score ▢

If you have ticked **2 or more** of the following, you may most likely have hypothyroid-related hair loss. Consult your trichologist.

Hypothyroidism (Too less thyroid hormone)

☐ Weight gain

☐ Constipation

☐ Sluggishness

☐ Fatigue; lack of energy

☐ Dry skin

☐ Depression

Your Test Score [ ]

A point worth noting is that, apart from diffuse hair loss all over the scalp, thyroid problems can also trigger patchy hair loss — alopecia areata. Smooth, bald patches may spontaneously appear over the scalp in this condition.

While hyperthyroidism causes general hair loss on the scalp, making hair thin and sparse, hypothyroidism makes hair dry, brittle, coarse and sparse, on the outer edge of the eyebrows.

In addition, general loss of body hair from areas other than the scalp may also sometimes be seen in thyroid disease.

DIAGNOSIS

Thyroid disease can trigger a number of symptoms which are helpful in diagnosis — some apparent, some subtle.

Your trichologist will order a simple blood test, when you present with symptoms that indicate thyroid disease — to confirm the diagnosis.

When the cause of hair loss due to thyroid disorders is established, the next step is to treat the hormonal problem — once this is done, hair loss automatically comes under control.

In most cases, once the hormones reach normal levels, excessive hair loss too comes under control. Likewise, the density or volume of hair which had reduced also comes back to 'normal.' However, this could take up to one hair cycle — i.e., over three years.

QUESTION TIME

Will my hair re-grow?

The chances for hair re-growth are not just bright, but excellent, once the underlying factor for hair loss — the thyroid problem — is adequately treated and thyroid levels are managed with medical treatment and appropriate dietetic and lifestyle measures.

Hyperthyroidism

➥ Make sure you eat broccoli, brussel sprouts, cabbage, cauliflower, kale, rutabagas, spinach, turnip, peaches and pears on a regular basis — they help to curb thyroid hormone production, naturally

➥ Avoid caffeinated drinks — they 'up' your anxiety levels and do no good to your thyroid problem.

Hypothyrodism

➡ Limit the intake of soy — it will do your hair and health no good, when your thyroid gland is underactive

➡ Use only iodised salt in your diet — it helps your thyroid

➡ Make fish, roasted sesame seeds, avocados and almonds, a part of your daily diet plan

➡ Exercise to keep fit and healthy

➡ Meditate to beat anxiety and stress.

OVARIAN CYSTS & HAIR

It's the ovary that maketh the woman.

Ovary is the female gonad. It is one of a pair of reproductive glands in women. The ovaries are located in the pelvis; one on each side of the uterus. Each ovary is about the size and shape of an almond.

The ovaries are the main source of female hormones (oestrogen) that control the development of female body characteristics, such as the breasts, body shape and body hair. They also regulate menstrual cycles and pregnancy.

Ovarian cysts, or polycystic ovary syndrome (pronounced *pah-lee-sis-tik oh-vuh-ree sin-drohm*), or PCOS, is a disorder in which a woman's hormones are 'out of balance.' The condition can cause problems with a woman's periods; it can also make it difficult to get pregnant.

Besides, PCOS may cause unwanted changes in the way a woman looks by way of appearance.

I've, in my practice, found PCOS to be rising in our country — we diagnose 1 in every 5 women who come to our clinics for hair loss treatment, having PCOS.

- PCOS is characterised by the build-up of numerous cysts in the ovaries, along with high testosterone (male hormone) levels, lack of ovulation and metabolic disturbances

- Many women with PCOS suffer from excessive hair growth on their faces, or other parts of their body, as a result of a condition called 'hirsutism.' On the other hand, they experience hair loss on the scalp — pattern baldness

- PCOS often manifests in one's teenage years. Nearly 10-12 per cent of women may be affected with PCOS worldwide. Women with PCOS tend to have irregular menses. The periods may sometimes stop.

While the exact cause of PCOS is not precisely known, it is evidenced that an imbalance in the endocrine system is to blame for many of the changes associated with PCOS. On the bright side, it is possible to treat hair loss, caused by PCOS with appropriate medical intervention.

Tell-tale Signs

(Tick box to do your own test)

If you have ticked **2 or more** of the following, you may most likely have PCOS-related hair loss. Consult your trichologist.

☐ Female pattern hair loss

☐ Excess hair growth (hirsutism) on the face, side-locks, and on forearms

☐ Irregular periods

☐ Difficulty to conceive

☐ Acne (pimples)

☐ Weight gain; difficult to reduce weight

☐ Irregular periods. About 30 per cent of women with PCOS present with this symptom

☐ Depression and mood swings.

Your Test Score ☐

Causes

➤ When levels of oestrogen in the body fall below normal, this disturbs the delicate hormonal balance in the body. In the process, it 'ups' the testosterone level and effects. The result is more 'masculine' features, such as increased body hair, coarse facial hair and pattern hair loss on the head

➤ Ovarian cysts, along with an underlying thyroid problem (most often hypothyroidism), often contribute to hair loss and weight problems.

DIAGNOSIS

PCOS often goes undiagnosed because many women often resort to using various home and other remedies to treat their facial hair gain and hair loss on the scalp without knowing the precise cause of the problem.

Excess hair has virtually led to laser therapy boom — so much so, laser treatment to 'ease-out hair' is a booming, million-dollar industry today.

PCOS is diagnosed with the following tests —

- Pelvic ultrasonography

- Oestrogen levels

- Testosterone levels

- FSH and LH

TREATMENT

The good news is that PCOS is treatable and shows good long-term response to treatment. Once the cysts shrink and the hormonal balance of the body is restored, hair loss automatically comes under control. It must be noted, however, that all the lost hair may not be regained. Excess loss of hair can be positively controlled, though. Even in cases where the cysts do not shrink completely, treatment can help to prevent worsening of hair loss.

CASE ILLUSTRATION

Twenty-nine-year-old Mita (name changed) came to us for hair loss on her scalp, coarse hair on her face, irregular periods and infertility. We lost no time in ordering a pelvic ultrasound (USG) for her. The USG confirmed polycystic ovarian syndrome (PCOS) — the most common form of hormonal disorder in women of reproductive age, which leads to hair loss on the scalp and hair growth in areas that ought to not have hair.

We prescribed her a suitable homeopathic remedy, based on her symptom-picture. As the treatment progressed, it not only helped ease her PCOS symptoms, but also helped to stabilise her hair loss. After 8-10 months of homeopathic treatment, a repeat USG showed she was cured of PCOS; her hair loss was also under control.

For more patient testimonials, visit — http://www.youtube.com/drbatrasgroup

➡ Be active. Exercise regularly. Exercise 'ups' your metabolism and helps you manage your PCOS symptoms better

➡ Avoid processed foods, because they contain chemicals, additives and artificial colourings. They worsen your PCOS symptoms and also hair loss

➡ Avoid sugar, fruit-soda juice and refined carbohydrates; they affect insulin resistance

➟ Avoid cold foods and ice-cold drinks; they take longer to go through the digestive tract; they also slow down your body's metabolism. Remember, individuals with PCOS often have sluggish metabolism

➟ Avoid alcohol and smoking. Smoking and alcohol can cause hair loss. They also affect hormonal balance and fertility — a consequence of PCOS

➟ Add flaxseed and soy to your diet — flaxseed is good for hair loss, while soy is good for hormonal 'balance' and hair loss.

PREGNANCY, CHILDBIRTH AND HAIR

It is rightly said that a child gives birth to a mother.

Ah, the joys of motherhood... Nothing is more blissful for a woman than to be in the family way. Pregnancy and the birth of a child makes a woman feel complete.

Pregnancy is a time when a host of biological and emotional changes occur in the body, as it prepares itself to nurture a new life.

What also impacts, or factors, a woman's hair is a rise in the level of the female hormone, oestrogen.

This is the 'upside' during pregnancy. It happens because oestrogen causes hair to remain in the growing phase; it also stimulates hair growth.

Many expectant mothers have gorgeous, healthy, luxurious hair on the scalp. Their hair literally blossoms like a flower during this time.

TRESS HIGH

When high levels of oestrogen maintain hair in the growth phase, hair falls out much less in pregnancy as compared to any other time. In addition, the hair strands also get stronger and grow longer. This gets all the more accentuated during the last trimester. No surprise, therefore, that many women sport glowing skin and beautiful, lustrous hair during this time.

CHILDBIRTH

Things change once the baby is born. The oestrogen levels that were high during pregnancy come sharply down to normal — and, hair moves from the growing phase to the falling phase. This is normal. In certain cases, it's this stark contrast between hair growth in pregnancy and hair loss post-delivery that often alarms some women.

Post-delivery hair loss may sometimes continue for 6-9 months. It does not need medical treatment — a good, nutritious diet that supplements the body with optimal amounts of iron, vitamins, minerals and proteins, is adequate. It can take up to a year to re-grow the hair lost after delivery.

DIAGNOSIS

Post-delivery hair loss requires no special tests for diagnosis. However, if it continues for a longer period than expected, or if hair density, or thickness, does not seem to improve in spite of proper diet, check for the following:

- Haemoglobin
- Serum Ferritin

Your trichologist may prescribe iron or folic acid supplements, when iron deficiency is detected.

Consume an iron-rich diet —

➥ Dark green leafy vegetables (spinach; collards)

➥ Egg yolk, red meat and liver

➥ Dried fruits (prunes; raisins; apricots)

➥ Beans, lentils, chick peas and dates

➥ Fortified breakfast cereals.

MENOPAUSE AND HAIR

The word, menopause, refers to the permanent stoppage of periods (menses), which generally occurs between age 45 and 50. Some women accept this change of life without worries; others, owing to myths attached to the expected process and hormonal changes, develop anxiety and also emotional upheaval.

Over 50 per cent of women going through menopause experience significant hair loss.

Tell-tale Signs

(Tick box to do your own test)

If you have ticked **2 or more** of the following, you may most likely have menopause-related hair loss. Consult your trichologist.

☐ Noticeable frontal thinning of scalp hair by age 50

☐ Emotional and psychological effects of hair loss, leading to lowered self-esteem, social anxiety — and, also reduced job performance

☐ Anxiety, mood swings, hot flashes and irritability

☐ Unusual levels of stress with sleep loss.

Your Hair Score ☐

Causes

➤ Changes in hormone levels (loss of oestrogen and progesterone)

➤ Increased testosterone

➤ Stress (physical or emotional)

➤ Certain medications, scalp and dermatological issues and heredity.

Put simply, a drop in the levels of the female hormones, progesterone and oestrogen, during menopause tends to put the hair in a prolonged resting phase. Hair loss at menopause tends to get worse for women who have a family history of hair loss.

➥ Drink green tea, get enough vitamin B6, lose weight, and use a hyaluronic acid-based shampoo. They may help restore some hair growth in 3-4 months

➥ Beat stress. Get adequate sleep, exercise regularly, and use relaxation techniques, such as meditation and deep breathing. They can help ease your hair loss and other menopause-related symptoms, such as anxiety

➥ Add soy foods to your diet. Soy-isoflavones have oestrogenic effects, without the risk or side-effects of synthetic hormone replacement therapy (HRT). They have been clinically proven to treat hair loss in women.

ANAEMIA AND HAIR

HAIR-FILE

Tea contains tannin, which interferes with iron absorption.

Hence, tea must be avoided for at least an hour after eating a meal.

Statistics suggests that 60 per cent of women in India, who complain of hair loss, suffer from iron-deficiency anaemia.

Whatever the cause of hair loss in men and women, it is definitely worsened by iron-deficiency anaemia. In fact, most of my patients who suffer from hair loss are screened for iron-deficiency as part of preliminary investigations.

Though it may occur in men too, iron-deficiency anaemia is more common in women. The reasons for this may be summarised as follows:

➤ Losing blood by way of monthly periods (in women)

➤ Eating food that may not be rich in dietary iron

➤ Going on 'crash diets' to attain, or remain in shape

➤ Early menarche (onset of periods) is one common reason for anaemia in young girls in India today

➤ Poor absorption of iron in diet even if diet is nutritious.

In my practice, I have seen that in women who are premenopausal or don't have any other complaints, such as ovarian cysts (PCOS), iron-deficiency anaemia is one of the prime reasons for hair loss.

Tell-tale Signs

(Tick box to do your own test)

If you have ticked **1 or more** of the following, you may most likely have anaemia-related hair loss. Consult your trichologist.

☐ There may be a lot of shedding of hair

☐ In some cases, hair loss may be subtle where hair has thinned out over a period of months/years

☐ Hair may be dry or brittle

☐ Heavy periods.

Your Hair Score [　　　　]

Causes

➤ Hair follicles contain ferritin — the protein that stores iron. Whenever there is iron-deficiency in the body, ferritin from the hair follicles is moved and used up for more essential body functions

➤ Lack of ferritin in the hair follicles affects the hair's ability to grow.

DIAGNOSIS

This can be easily done by way of following tests:

• Complete blood count

• Serum ferritin levels

- Stool test (to check for loss of blood via stools).

TREATMENT

Replenishing the iron stores in the body with the help of iron supplements is the answer. Your trichologist will advise you on which supplement to take and the dosage. Remember, self-treatment may be dangerous, or damaging.

→ Consume a diet rich in iron, such as red meat, dried fruits (raisins; figs), iron-fortified cereals, dark-green leafy vegetables, beans, liver and egg yolk

→ Include a good amount of proteins in your diet, because protein is essential for replenishing ferritin stores in your body.

TOXIC ELEMENTS, PRESCRIPTION DRUGS & HAIR

It's a dirty, dirty world out there — you name it, pollutants in the air, toxins or heavy metals. They are part of our environment and elsewhere. Did you know that even our household products and electronic gadgets are not exempt from making us ill, or losing hair?

Aluminium, arsenic, cadmium, lead and mercury — not to speak of nickel and iron — are elements we are all exposed to on a daily basis. Other 'offenders' include certain conventional medications, hygiene products, foodstuff, cosmetics, air and water.

It is agreed that certain trace elements, such as iron, or selenium, are required in small quantities for health. However, any excess, or too much of a 'good' thing, is an invite for trouble.

WARNING Hair loss is one major 'fallout' of metal toxicity. Hair loss can occur for a variety of reasons, including exposure to the following —

☛ Do you know that arsenic, used in glass manufacturing, metal refining, silicon chip manufacturing, insecticides, rat poisons, fungicides and wood preservatives, can trigger hair loss?

☛ That mercury toxicity from consumption of mercury-containing seafood and also from exposure to mercury-containing medications, paint, fungicides and industrial products, can lead to hair loss?

☛ That boric acid, a popular 'must-use' on your carrom board, can cause hair loss when unintentionally 'ingested' over a period of time?

☛ That chlorine in our water supply, or swimming pools, could be yet another cause of hair loss?

Medical tests are the only way to determine whether metal toxicity is the cause of hair loss. This is performed by measuring 'trace elements' content of hair — to figure out health problems due to deficiencies or excesses of minerals.

Hair is a mirror of health and illness — it has a long history of successful use in detecting long-term exposure or outcomes to toxic heavy metals.

The reason is simple — hair 'concentrates' heavy metals several times more than concentrations in blood.

Remember! High levels of toxicity in hair may reflect early or chronic exposure and elevations, following exposure. Some examples —

🪮 *Environmental or Job-related Exposure.* Examples include chemical, painting, printing and welding industry

🪮 *Use of Certain Products.* Examples include hair colouring treatments, paint and ink

🪮 *Gut-related Issues.* Examples include long-standing digestive disorders, dietetic excess, undernourishment and prolonged or indiscriminate use of antibiotics and other prescription drugs.

In some cases, hair loss may be 'toxicity-induced.' Examples include metal salts and heavy metals — copper, lithium, thallium and gold. They cause hair loss, as a result of prolonged exposure, or by ingestion.

CAUSE & EFFECT

Environmental toxins and certain conventional medications can, in the short- or long-term, contribute to hair loss.

Such substances cause hair loss by disrupting basic cellular functions in the body. Certain drugs, for instance, can also stop re-growth of hair follicles.

Symptoms

1. Hair loss (may be localised or widespread)

2. Allergies

3. Skin problems

4. Loss of co-ordination

5. Numbness and tingling in the limbs

6. Mood-related problems

7. Joint pain

8. Swelling

9. Chronic fatigue

10. Cognitive problems — such as difficulty with memory, planning, foresight and judgment

Speak to your trichologist, if you have 3 or more of the above symptoms, because early diagnosis and treatment offer the best preventative and therapeutic outcomes for hair loss.

Management

People in careers, like mining or plastics manufacture, are at a greater risk for toxicity and hair loss. Speak to your trichologist, if you have such job profiles or concerns about health and hair loss.

To confirm diagnosis, your trichologist will order hair analysis, along with blood and urine tests.

PRESCRIPTION DRUGS

Remember!

Many common prescription drugs — even certain popular OTC products — can cause hair loss.

- Steroidal medications; non-steroidal anti-inflammatory drugs (NSAIDs; e.g., *nimesulide*); other anti-inflammatory drugs (*acetaminophen/paracetamol*) and arthritis drugs (*methotrexate*, also used for psoriasis)

- Drugs (*accutane*), for acne, derived from vitamin A, or other skin conditions

- Birth control (oral contraceptive) pills (*Mala D, Ovral*) and all hormone-containing drugs prescribed for hormone-related, reproductive, male- and female-specific conditions, such as HRT and anabolic steroids

- Anti-hypertensives, to reduce high blood pressure, such as beta-blockers (*atenolol*)

- Blood thinners (anti-coagulants), such as *aspirin* or *warfarin*

- Drugs for indigestion, stomach disorders and ulcers, including *cimetidine* and *ranitidine*

- Drugs used to treat thyroid problems (*synthroid, levoxyl*)

- Anti-fungal creams and lotions (*clotrimazole*)

- Anti-depression drugs, such as *Prozac*

- *Statins*, or cholesterol-lowering drugs

- Anti-epileptic drugs, such as *trimethadione*

- Levadopa (*dopar; larodopa*), for Parkinson's disease

🛉 Chemotherapy, and chemotherapeutic drugs, used in the treatment of cancer.

Note: If a conventional medication or drug is found to be the cause, a change of medication, or dose, may be helpful to control hair loss. This should not be done without consulting your doctor.

'TOXIC BOMB' WAITING TO EXPLODE IN YOUR ELECTRONIC GADGET

Lead from consumer electronics make up almost 40 per cent of what is being continually dumped into landfills and scrap yards. An average computer uses 4 lb of lead, which approximates 6 per cent of the total weight of a standard PC. Your PC screen may contain 2-5 gm of lead.

Cadmium is part of resistors, infrared detectors, semi-conductors, some older versions cathode ray tubes, photocopiers, batteries etc., Cadmium is an extremely toxic metal — it can cause irreversible health problems. It is primarily absorbed through breathing.

Barium is another potential hazard. It is used in the front panel of certain gadgets to protect users from radiation. Barium can affect through air, water, soil and also fish. Research says that even relatively insignificant or short-term exposure to barium can result in brain affections, muscle weakness and damage to the heart, liver and spleen.

Mercury poses a dangerous threat to our health. Approximately 20 per cent of the annual world consumption of mercury is used in electrical and electronic equipment. Mercury is used in PC and liquid crystal (LCD) flat screens. These screens, as you'd know, also contain lead. A powerful poison, mercury, in small amounts, is more toxic than lead, cadmium and even arsenic. Although mercury forms a small part of your PC (0.0022 per cent), it is still a health risk.

Among other equally dangerous toxins 'waiting to explode' in your PC, or other gadgets, are tin, arsenic, chromium, selenium, manganese and silver, not to speak of stabilisers and additives in food products.

STRESS & HAIR

Happiness has an emotional bounce — it adds a bright, shiny look to our overall confidence and also behaviour. It 'pumps' zest to everything we do, including our hair.

Stress has just the opposite effect.

No one is exempt from the manifold pressures and stresses of life. Some of us cope with stresses well, while some allow them to run riot and create serious trouble for themselves and also for others around them.

Stress is, in actuality, an infinite process. Think of it — peer pressure, business competition and danger lurking around the corner, or fear of the unknown, social taboo or tensions. These are issues and also reactions that cannot be put under the lid or 'purged' easily.

Our day-to-day life too has its allocation of stress: marital, financial and workplace problems. If there were no human resilience, stress would have probably knocked us out, or made us as dead as the dodo!

The fact is our psyche is so stunningly 'engineered' that some stresses are managed well, while some are yielded to, or accepted. Besides, one sort of manages to live with them, till one 'breaks' down in the wake of stressful hopelessness.

The effect of stress on hair loss has been known for a long time.

While it is natural to lose about 50-100 strands of hair each day, there is reason for us to worry when our hair thins, or falls, in clumps, or small bald patches appear.

When this happens, you'd think of stress as a factor affecting your health and, in turn, your hair.

Tell-tale Signs

(Tick box to do your own hair loss 'stress' test)

If you have ticked **3 or more** of the following, along with hair loss, you may most likely have stress symptoms. Consult your trichologist.

- ☐ Feel irritable

- ☐ Anxious

- ☐ Low self-esteem

- ☐ Mood changes; low mood

- ☐ Have racing thoughts

- ☐ Worry constantly

- ☐ Imagine that something worse is going to happen

- ☐ Lose your temper easily

- ☐ Drink more; smoke more

- ☐ Talk fast, or go out often

- ☐ Change in your eating habits

- ☐ Isolate yourself; not socialise

- ☐ Are forgetful or awkward

- ☐ Are impetuous; act hastily

- ☐ Have difficulty to concentrate or focus

Your Stress Score [ ]

STRESS EFFECT

Stress, according to scientific research, affects our body in more ways than one. It affects our nervous, endocrine (hormonal) and also immune systems.

When stress disturbs balance or harmony in any of the three systems, they do not function at their best. This can have profound health consequences — from hair loss to a host of other illnesses.

Stress-triggered hair loss is generally short-term, or temporary. It is profound when the stressor exists, or is continually present.

Once the stress factor is reduced, there is often re-growth, although the process can take up to six months, or more — provided there is no other stress factor waiting to 'detonate.'

Remember! Chronic, or extreme, stress for long periods can cause substantial damage to your hair, sometimes leading to permanent baldness.

Causes

Chronic, or prolonged periods of stress like illness, divorce, death of a loved one, job loss, surgical stress, or accidents can trigger temporary hair loss. It can stop hair from growing. After a few months, the hair falls out and is not replaced.

Why does this happen? Severe stress can cause the growing hair follicles to prematurely move into the regression phase and, thereafter, the resting phase, during which the hair fall out uneventfully.

The shedding may not be apparent for the first few weeks; but, when it occurs suddenly, it becomes obvious. This may occur as a delayed response, so it is often a 'hairy' catch-22 situation for the person suffering from the condition.

What compounds the problem is the stressful event *per se* is often forgotten. It is also seldom connected with the 'new' dilemma — hair loss.

The end result is a scalp showing hair loss.

"I'm Pulling My Hair Out" (Trichotillomania)

A rather strange type of hair loss results from compulsive, or compelling, hair pulling. This is a psychological disorder. It is called trichotillomania (TTM) — *tricho* for hair and *mania* for such a 'self-inflicted' fad.

It most often affects women more than men. It also affects young children and teenagers, most often girls than boys — primarily in response to anxiety, peer and parental pressure. Sometimes, the affected individual may also eat their hair!

Tell-tale Signs

(Tick box below to do your own test)

If you have ticked **2 or more** of the following, you may most likely have trichotillomania. Consult your trichologist.

☐   Repeated pulling one's own hair out, typically from scalp, eyebrows or eyelashes

☐   A strong urge to pull hair — this gives relief or comfort from anxiety or stress

☐   Patchy bald areas on the scalp or other areas of your body

☐   Thin or missing eyelashes or eyebrows

☐   Chewing or eating pulled-out hair

☐   Playing with pulled-out hair.

Your Hair Score [   ]

Hair loss is stopped once the hair pulling obsession is controlled and treated.

TREATMENT

Cutting the hair short, to make 'pulling' extremely difficult, is useful as an 'interim' quick-fix.

Counselling, along with emotional and family support, is imperative. Medical treatment is aimed at treating the underlying factor and also stress.

Fortunately, once pulling and tugging of hair stops, hair can grow back again, because TTM is a temporary form of hair loss.

CASE ILLUSTRATION

Eighteen-year-old Sushmita (name changed) presented with hair loss. Her mother reported, with obvious distress, that Sushmita was losing "a lot of hair for the past 3-4 months." We analysed and also did a video microscopy test and found that Sushmita's hair loss was caused by trichotillomania — pulling out hair on purpose.

After we heard her mother's 'plea' to help stop her daughter's hair loss, we spoke to Sushmita separately. To begin with, she was unwilling to 'talk' about her problem. Slowly, she began to open up. She said that she always wanted to study engineering, but her parents were forcing her to opt for medicine, for which she had no liking or interest. She reported that this was a terrifying 'subject' of discussion, everyday, at the dinner table. She said that she could not bear her parents' constant pressure tactics, nagging and the like. To get over her stress, there was nothing else she'd think of, except pulling her own hair — a practice which she said gave her emotional relief, or outlet to getting over her nerves, or angst.

We counselled her and put her on an appropriate homeopathic medicine. It wasn't long before her 'hair pulling' episodes stopped and she regained her lost hair.

For more patient testimonies, visit — http://www.youtube.com/drbatrasgroup

ILLNESS & HAIR

Certain illnesses cause hair loss because of a confused and over-active immune system. As if the primary problem itself was not annoying or draining enough, hair loss further adds to one's woes. Such illnesses may 'shock' the body and this pushes a lot of hair prematurely into the 'resting phase' after which they fall off.

 Some of the common illnesses that trigger hair loss are —

🔸 Malaria

🔸 Typhoid

🔸 Jaundice

🔸 Cholera

🔸 High fever, due to any other causes (viral or bacterial infection).

Apart from the above acute problems, hair loss may also be triggered by the following —

🔸 Post-heart attack

🔸 After undergoing major surgery

🔸 Chronic illnesses such as lupus; chronic bowel disorders

🔸 Anaemia

🔸 Thyroid disorders

🔸 Psoriasis

🔸 Diabetes

Causes

Hair loss generally becomes noticeable 6-12 weeks after illness. This is because once the body encounters illness, it 'shocks' the hair and moves them from a phase of growth into a phase of rest.

➡ *Timely Treatment.* Although it's natural to lose hair after such illnesses, it's vital to treat it properly, and, in time, so that the lost hair re-grows. If left untreated, one is often left behind with scanty and thinned out hair

➡ *Adequate Nutrition.* A healthy, balanced diet is important for recovering from such hair loss

➡ *De-stress.* Although it may be stressful to watch hair strands coming off in handfuls, it is necessary to keep stress under control and accept such hair loss after illness as a normal process. Taking appropriate measures, under the guidance of a trichologist, will help you to come out of the state in a few months

➡ *Hair Care.* Avoid chemical treatments, hair colours, blow dryers, hair ironing, tight hairstyles, and procedures that may damage your hair. Use a mild, natural shampoo and condition regularly

➡ *Supplements.* Speak to your trichologist about the right food and dietary supplements that 'suit' your individual needs or requirements.

CANCER & HAIR

The word, cancer, brings nothing but a sense of surging fear to anyone's mind.

The expression was first introduced by Hippocrates. He used the words *carcinos* (meaning, crab) and *carcinoma* to describe cellular growths. He decided to call cancer 'crab,' because of its appearance. Most of the cancers that Hippocrates detected were end-stage cancers. Today, with technological advances, screening programmes, early detection and treatment, things have changed to a large extent, albeit cancer still holds a gloomy, 'ghost-like' grip in one's mind.

CHEMO-EFFECT

Remember!

Hair loss is a potential side-effect of chemotherapy and radiation therapy for cancer. Hair loss may occur throughout the body, including the head, face, arms, legs, underarms, and pubic area, after chemotherapy. The amount of hair loss may depend on the type of chemotherapy drug used and the dosage. Most often, hair begins to fall 2-3 weeks after chemotherapy.

If you are undergoing chemotherapy it is likely that all your hair will fall out.

Why Hair Falls

Chemotherapy is basically targeted at rapidly growing cells in the body, because cancer cells multiply and grow rapidly. However, hair, being one of the fastest growing tissues, also becomes the 'unfortunate target' of chemotherapy/drugs. The result is hair loss from all over the body.

Hair loss, related to cancer treatment, is generally short-term. In most cases, hair will grow back. Hair re-growth, after chemotherapy, usually begins a month or two after chemotherapy is stopped.

It may take 6-12 months for complete hair re-growth to be established. However, when new hair grows, its texture and density may be different from the hair that was earlier lost. The colour of re-grown hair may also differ from the original, natural hair.

RADIATION

Radiation therapy affects the hair located within the field of radiation. Hair typically returns in the area of radiation therapy after some months. It may be thinner and appear with a different texture than the original hair.

When high doses of radiation are used to treat cancer, the hair may not re-grow in the area where radiation therapy was given.

TREATMENT

While you are preparing for cancer treatment, it may be worthwhile considering options to cover up the baldness that is imminent. Wigs can be a good option for men as well as women. Tying a scarf around the head can be another simple option for women.

Homeopathic treatment is a natural, holistic way to deal with the side-effects of conventional cancer treatment. Homeopathic remedies antidote the harmful effects of cancer treatment and make your journey through the treatment less discomforting.

This reminds me of one of my patients who had lost all her hair due to cancer treatment. Besides having to deal with her depression related to cancer, she was also suffering from 'balding blues.' This was only adding to her misery. I prescribed her the homeopathic remedy, *Nux Vomica*, which not only helped her to deal with the side-effects of cancer drugs, but also stimulated re-growth of hair.

SCIENTIFIC EVALUATION OF HAIR LOSS

Hair is a 'temple' of surprises. It tells a lot about our persona from the point-of-view of both health and illness.

You can't figure out what lies behind the beauty of a blooming flower without examining it from the inside-out. Likewise, hair — its 'hidden secrets' can only be figured out with state-of-the-art scientific diagnostic tests, while going far beyond what appears on the surface. This is not only helpful from the analytical, but also from the preventative and treatment standpoint.

PC-BASED VIDEO-MICROSCOPY

The PC-based video microscope is an advanced electronic imaging system — I call it "a trichologist's best friend." It allows the trichologist to evaluate the condition of the hair and scalp, which is evidently visible on the computer screen.

The best part is that even patients can watch their scalp under high magnification on the screen.

Nothing can be more exciting than watching 'live' what the trichologist perceives — seeing, after all, is believing!

USES

- Helps identify your type of hair loss
- Can identify the thickness of your hair strands and how densely packed your hair is

- Detects early thinning of hair and reduced hair density

- Can easily pick up widened gaps between hair

- Can predict hair loss much before the problem becomes evident

- Determines scalp health; detects dandruff, or other conditions affecting the scalp.

ADVANTAGES

⚬ Non-invasive test (magnifies your scalp 200 times its size)

⚬ Images/videos can be captured and saved on the computer

⚬ It's an excellent way to record detailed 'before-and-after' images of patients

⚬ It is also used during hair transplantation procedure for preparing grafts and during graft placement

⚬ Helps determine scalp type so the 'right' kind of shampoo can be recommended

⚬ Helps to demonstrate hair re-growth to patients following hair transplantation.

Needless to say, video microscopy test is an invaluable tool to diagnose hair and scalp problems and provide in-depth analysis to patients.

TRICHOSCAN

TrichoScan is yet another advanced tool. It holds a prime place in trichology. TrichoScan was invented by my friend, Professor Dr Rolf Hoffman. It was first introduced in India, by me, in 2006.

TrichoScan is, indeed, the world's first-ever technological tool to monitor hair density and 'measure' effectiveness of treatment.

Earlier, the problem in the field of trichology was that results were not measurable.

The introduction of TrichoScan has brought about a revolution in the field — it can scientifically measure and document, or validate, treatment outcomes. It is basically a software-based method for the analysis of human hair. The procedure involves taking magnified digital images of the scalp with a specially developed camera-optics system. The software is, thereafter, used to automatically calculate important parameters from these images, such as density of hair or the number of hair in a given area.

USES

- Offers computerised calculation of your hair density or thickness (It has special lens attached to a camera)

- Diagnoses pattern hair loss even before the thinning can be appreciated by the naked eye

- Helps to measure treatment efficacy (by comparing 'before-after' hair density and thickness)

- Detects scalp problems like dandruff, seborrhoea and psoriasis

- It can actually help to count the number of hair on your head!

- Can also detect actual rate of hair growth.

TrichoScan is a patient-friendly, inexpensive, effective and reliable means for diagnosing hair problems. It is, by far, the only tool for hair measurement that has been validated by an external scientific body. Its accuracy is pegged at a whopping 99.8 per cent. TrichoScan also helps in avoiding painful procedures like a scalp biopsy. However, the downside is that the test requires shaving a patch (about one inch in diameter) on your scalp.

HAIR ANALYSIS

Hair analysis is a procedure in which a small sample of hair is used to assess an individual's health. Hair is one of the fastest growing tissues in the body; it contains almost all the minerals present in the body.

Hence, a detailed analysis of hair can provide valuable information about bodily functions and its nutritional status, over a period of time.

SIGNIFICANCE

A blood test generally indicates the 'current quantity' of minerals in your body, based on what you've consumed, recently. Hair analysis, on the other hand, will provide an insight into the body stores of that mineral over a period of time; it detects if you are deficient in it, or have excess, too. For example, your potassium may be high after eating a banana vis-à-vis a blood test, but hair analysis may show that your body is deficient in potassium.

Hair Mineral Analysis: What it Can Tell

Common Conditions	Common Mineral Imbalances	Mineral Toxicities
Hyperthyroidism	Sodium	Lead
Hypothyroidism	Potassium	Arsenic
Pre-diabetes/Diabetes	Calcium	Beryllium
Moderate/severe nutritional deficiencies	Phosphorus	Cadmium
Adrenal dysfunction	Magnesium	Aluminium
	Iron	Nickel

Test results, however, may be affected by the type and condition of hair, as well as the individual's age and sex.

Hair analysis has a high rate of accuracy, much more than urine and blood tests — although certain factors are likely to affect its accuracy. This includes:

- The area from which hair is taken

- Environmental factors: where you live and work affects your exposure to chemicals and toxins

- The use of powerful, chemical-based hair products

- Rate of hair growth.

This is one reason why multiple tests are usually done, every few months, to follow-up on the individual's health and to determine whether both diagnosis and treatment have led to the reduction of a disease or illness, or not.

BLOOD TESTS

Blood tests are useful to find out the cause of your hair loss. Your trichologist, of course, will recommend relevant tests — to find out the underlying factor, if any, and institute appropriate treatment.

HORMONAL IMBALANCE

- *TSH* (thyroid stimulating hormone) test for hormonal problems, such as thyroid disorders

- *FSH* (follicle stimulating hormone) test for women reaching menopause

- A detailed *hormonal assay* may sometimes be ordered by your trichologist, if hormonal imbalance is suspected.

NUTRITIONAL DEFICIENCIES

- *Ferritin:* Too little of iron can be a cause of hair loss and this can be easily picked up by a blood test

- *Complete blood count* (CBC) may provide 'pointers' towards other causes of hair loss, such as folic acid and vitamin B12 deficiency, so also infections and cancer.

OTHER TESTS

- *Blood sugar test* (fasting and post-lunch) may be required to check for diabetes

- *Electrolyte imbalance,* if suspected, can be confirmed or ruled out by blood tests

- *FANA* (fluorescent antinuclear antibody) test, for certain conditions like alopecia areata may be required.

GENETIC HAIR TEST

The first-ever genetic hair test for androgenetic alopecia, or male pattern baldness, came into vogue in 2008. The test 'screens' changes in the androgen receptor gene on the X chromosome, the gene associated with male pattern hair loss. The aim of the test is to identify individuals at augmented risk of developing hair loss before it is clinically evident — so that medical treatment can be started early, when it is most effective. It may, however, be emphasised that there is, at present, just a 'likely' conjecture with the gene cited and hair loss. The association has not yet been conclusively proved.

HAIR PULL TEST

In this test, a group of hair (approximately 40-60 hairs) is gently pulled — starting from the front of the scalp to the back, in 5-6 different areas of scalp.

The pull test is done for evaluation of scalp hair loss. Normally, less than three hair strands come out with each pull from each area; if more than 5 hair strands come out with every pull or approximately ten per cent of pulled hairs come out, the pull test is considered 'positive.' The individual should not shampoo or wash hair for 24-48 hours prior to the test for accurate results to emerge.

The hair pull test is useful for the following —

- To see which areas of your scalp are more prone to hair loss

- How many hair come out with each pull indicates the severity of your hair loss problem

- It's also used to judge the progress of the individual with treatment. Hair pull will reduce to normal with effective treatment.

SCALP BIOPSY

When the cause of hair loss is unidentified, undiagnosed, or is not known, your trichologist may order a scalp biopsy.

This is a short procedure performed, by a technician, under local anaesthesia. A small area of the scalp, where the biopsy is to be taken, is 'frozen' or 'numbed' with a needle. The sample, which is placed in formalin to preserve, is sent for laboratory analysis. It may take 1-4 weeks to get biopsy results. A biopsy is rarely used except when diagnosis is unclear.

GLOBAL PHOTOGRAPHY

A photograph speaks more than a thousand words.

Photography is a good way to judge and monitor treatment on the basis of 'before' and 'after' photographs.

However, one should make sure —

- To keep the camera, its angle and focus at the same level

- To keep their hair dry, while retaining the same hairstyle, hair length and colour.

CONVENTIONAL MEDICAL TREATMENT OF HAIR LOSS

Certain types of hair loss are temporary. Hair may re-grow without any treatment. In most conditions, treatment will be required to help promote hair growth or hide latent or apparent hair loss.

For most types of hair loss, especially when hair loss is caused by an underlying disease, treatment is necessary — not to just stall hair loss, but also control further loss.

Drug	Mode of Use	Effects	Time Duration	Side-effects
Minoxidil	Applied locally. Lotion or foam (2%-5%)	• Promotes hair growth in the area where it is applied	• Effects often begin within 2-4 months of application • Effects end soon after stopping the drug	• Unwanted facial/ body hair • Local allergic reaction/s • Fast or irregular heartbeat
Finasteride	Taken orally as tablet	• Slows down hair loss • Stimulates hair growth	• Effects (less hair loss) are commonly seen after 3-4 months of regular treatment • It takes 6-12 months to see thickening and strengthening of hair in a small %age of patients • Effects end on stopping the drug • There may be rebound 'excess' hair loss after stopping	• Erectile dysfunction (ED) or impotence • Decreased sex drive • Reduced ejaculate amount • Breast enlargement in men

MINOXIDIL

Minoxidil was originally developed as a tablet for treating high blood pressure. It was found to have a number of side-effects, including hair growth on the face and other non-hairy areas of the body. This made minoxidil a useful drug for treating hair loss.

Minoxidil is used as a local application on the scalp.

The original studies on minoxidil were performed on the crown (top) of the head, where it works best. The downside is — it doesn't work if the area is totally bald. Effects are best visible between six months to two years after treatment. Thereafter, you may see a gradual decrease in effectiveness.

Minoxidil is FDA-approved for use by men and women — the only hair re-growth ingredient approved by the FDA for use by the latter.

 **Side-effects**

☛ Burning, stinging, or redness at the application site

☛ Unwanted facial and body hair, dizziness, fast or irregular heartbeats, fainting spells, chest pain, swelling of hands and feet, and hypotension

☛ Allergic reaction, including rash, itching or swelling (especially of the face, tongue and throat), severe dizziness and trouble while breathing.

FINASTERIDE (PROSCAR)

The drug finasteride (Proscar used in prostate enlargement) was approved for use in male pattern balding in 1998. It has been formulated as an oral tablet.

Finasteride blocks the formation of dihydrotestosterone (DHT) which is the hormone responsible for pattern hair loss. It is evidenced to control hair loss in a few cases, while it can help hair re-growth in a few cases. It is not approved for use by women.

 **Side-effects**

☞ Erectile dysfunction (ED) or impotence

☞ Decreased libido (sex drive)

☞ Decreased ejaculate amount

☞ Suicidal tendencies, according to a new study

☞ Breast enlargement in men

☞ Foetal defects

The most serious side-effect of finasteride use is birth defects that can occur if pregnant women are exposed to crushed or broken tablets. It specifically results in defects in the sex organs of male foetuses. Owing to the severity of this side-effect, finasteride is not recommended for use in men who want to father a child, or pregnant women, or those who can become pregnant in the future.

As a matter of fact, the risk is so enormous that pregnant women are advised not to even touch broken tablets of finasteride.

DUTASTERIDE

This is yet another conventional drug 'evidenced' to 'help' hair growth. There are no long-term term studies on its safety and efficacy in hair loss. However, short-term study results have been promising — with its DHT-inhibiting effects.

MEDICATIONS FOR WOMEN WITH HAIR LOSS

Topical applications, such as minoxidil, aid re-growth of hair or slow-down the progress of hair loss in women. In some instances, injectible topical medications accelerate re-growth of hair.

SPIRONOLACTONE

Spironolactone is an oral diuretic (or, water pill) that is suggested to help reduce unwanted hair in women. It has been studied in women with pattern hair loss — but with mixed results. It may have some effect in reducing hair thinning in women who present with limited pattern hair loss.

 Side-effects include bleeding from the gastrointestinal tract.

It is not used in men, because it can cause testicular atrophy and breast enlargement, aside from lowered sexual drive.

CYPROTERONE ACETATE

This drug has been used, with mixed results, in the treatment of hirsutism (excessive hair) as well as female pattern hair loss.

 The most likely serious side-effects are liver toxicity and increased rate of blood clots.

It may also be mentioned that oral contraceptive drugs play a vital role in controlling hair loss, in women, particularly certain OC pills which are predominantly high in oestrogen. OC pills prolong the growth phase of hair and make hair look stronger, grow longer and fall less. However, stopping OC pill use can bring about a 'rebound' increase in hair loss. Consult your trichologist, if you have such issues or concerns.

MANAGING EXPECTATIONS: What to Expect From Treatment

Most people expect miracles from prescription medications — blame it or praise it on advertising or media 'blitz.' It is imperative to 'weigh' out treatment outcomes — in other words, what topical (that you apply on your head) and oral medications can do for you. Remember, the hair you've lost years ago isn't likely to start growing quickly. Consider instead the idea of stopping excessive hair loss and, perhaps, experiencing some mild re-growth — you'd be happy with the results. Well, if your expectations are sky-high, disappointment is inevitable.

Having patience will help. Because, results take many months — not just days or weeks. Remember, hair grows slowly, so it will take a good deal of time before you notice any visible change.

Remember! Always follow your trichologist's advice and dosage. Stop medicine at your own risk — you will lose all benefits you may have gained from therapy. It will take one year for you to look your best in terms of your hair — better still, you will lose hair at a natural rate, not like before.

Thought the idea of gulping a pill or applying a solution is cumbersome? Don't think that way. Because, it is possible for new treatments to emerge and bring about better patient acceptance and also ease of use. Don't people take daily medications for chronic problems like high blood pressure or diabetes? It is all part of one's daily routine. It becomes a habit or practice — for health. This is true for hair loss prescription medications too.

OTHER TREATMENTS FOR HAIR LOSS

Dong Quai

Dong quai is one of the many herbs used in Traditional Chinese Medicine (TCM), primarily for relieving symptoms related to menopause. Many claim that Dong quai helps in controlling hair loss and stimulating hair re-growth, although this is not backed by scientific validation.

Serenoa Complex

Serenoa Complex is a drug that contains saw palmetto, vitamin E and zinc, besides other constituents. The drug is said to help re-growth of hair by blocking the effect of DHT hormone (the hormone responsible for hair loss). Again, there are neither clinical trials nor studies to back this claim fully.

Ayurveda for Hair Loss

Ayurveda is the ancient Indian medical science believed to be over 5,000 years old. The word ayurveda is derived from a combination of two Sanskrit words, *ayu* meaning 'life,' and *veda* meaning 'knowledge' or 'science.'

Some 'useful' remedies in ayurveda for hair loss are —

- *Bhringaraj* — Helps prevent hair loss as well as premature greying of hair

- *Gotu Kola* — Helps prevent hair loss as well as boost memory

- *Sandalwood* — Helps treat hair loss

- *Amalaki* — Helps prevent hair loss.

MESOTHERAPY

Mesotherapy (*mesos*, for 'middle,' and *therapeia*, 'to treat medically,' in Greek) is a non-surgical treatment. It employs multiple pharmaceutical and homeopathic agents, plant extracts, vitamins and other ingredients. Dr Michel Pistor (1924-2003), from France founded the field of mesotherapy, after diligent clinical research, in 1952.

Many of my patients were on a perennial quest — a new, painless procedure that could reduce the turnaround time for natural hair growth following effective medical treatment.

After having treated over 2,50,000 hair loss patients successfully, with the goodness of homeopathy and hair transplantation, at Dr Batra's Clinics, this idea bid fair for us to launch a pain-free, new procedure to stimulate such hair growth.

The procedure is called non-needle mesotherapy.

In the procedure, the principle of 'electroporation' is used, where pores of skin are opened using a heating system and therapeutic solutions — small quantities of natural extracts, homeopathic agents and vitamins — are allowed to penetrate the scalp. The pores are, thereafter, closed using a cooling system.

This promotes hair growth in the best turnaround time possible.

Types of Hair Loss that Can Be Treated with Mesotherapy

- Male and female pattern baldness

- Patchy hair loss

- Hair loss from stress or chronic illness (telogen effluvium)

However, it is imperative to evaluate one's health status and treat any underlying 'triggers' for hair loss, such as iron-deficiency anaemia, or thyroid problems, before undergoing the procedure. Because, successful treatment outcomes for hair loss depend on correcting the underlying 'cause,' or 'trigger.'

As a rule of the thumb, one would need ten sittings of non-needle mesotherapy — one sitting every week — for noticeable results to emerge. Although results usually become evident, after 4-5 weeks, it would be useful for one to continue with the procedure beyond the suggested schedule, for optimal treatment outcomes to emerge.

Remember! The only constraint is non-needle mesotherapy is not recommended in individuals having certain health conditions, such as:

- Kidney and liver disease

- Pregnancy and nursing

- For individuals having cardiac pacemaker.

However, what makes non-needle mesotherapy a boon for individuals suffering from hair loss is the procedure is not only painless, it is also free of side-effects. More importantly, there is no bleeding.

The procedure is not time-consuming — it takes just about half-an-hour for one to complete a session, or sitting.

Besides, the advantage of using homeopathic agents in non-needle mesotherapy is manifold. Homeopathic agents cause no allergy, or hypersensitivity. They integrate naturally and completely into the tissues and they have accredited safety parameters and also efficacy of use.

HOMEOPATHY

AT THE DOCTOR'S CLINIC

When patients visit the clinic for the first time, the homeopathic doctor takes an in-depth review of the individual's health status, his/her temperament, personality, likes and dislikes, sentiments and sensibilities. This is used to guide the selection of one, or more, homeopathic remedies.

This is supplemented by follow-up visits, where individuals report on how they are responding to the remedy, or remedies. This will help the doctor arrive at decisions about further treatment.

Homeopathy is, by far, the safest and most humane form of medical sciences. It aims to treat the whole person rather than just the physical, or apparent, symptoms.

Why is homeopathic treatment ideal for hair loss and other hair/scalp problems?

- *Free From Side-Effects.* Homeopathic medicines are free from side-effects. Not only do homeopathic remedies reduce hair loss, but they also protect the body from harmful effects (such as decreased libido, ejaculation problems) that are common with conventional drugs

- *Proven Effects.* Homeopathic remedies such as *Thuja Occidentalis* or *Sabal serrulata* have been used for treating hair loss in homeopathy for over 100 years. International clinical studies have proven that the two homeopathic remedies cited are natural DHT-inhibitors, i.e., they can control hair loss caused by DHT — without side-effects.

- *Mind-Body Medicine.* Homeopathy treats not only the physical complaints, but also targets the mind and gently restores mind-body equilibrium — thus, it treats patients as a 'whole.' This makes it an excellent solution for hair problems related to the mind, such as stress-related patchy hair loss (alopecia areata), hair-pulling disorder (trichotillomania), or stress-induced massive hair shedding

- *Verified by Studies.* A study conducted in Scotland revealed that 90 per cent of patients with patchy hair loss opted for homeopathy as the first choice of treatment. Homeopathy actually helps to slow down the progression of the bald patches and fill them up with new hair. A complete recovery is possible in most cases

- *Less Recurrence.* A detailed, long-term study conducted at **Dr Batra's** showed that the recurrence rate of patchy hair loss (alopecia areata) was just 9.1 per cent in patients treated with homeopathy, whereas it was as high as 50 per cent in patients who took conventional treatment for the disorder

- *Trusted Medicine.* An independent study conducted by **A C Nielsen** across five cities in India revealed that 90 per cent of patients taking homeopathy for their hair loss at **Dr Batra's** would not switch over to any other brand or treatment. This speaks for the credibility of homeopathic science and the faith our patients place in us.

Dr BATRA'S 'HEADY' STORY

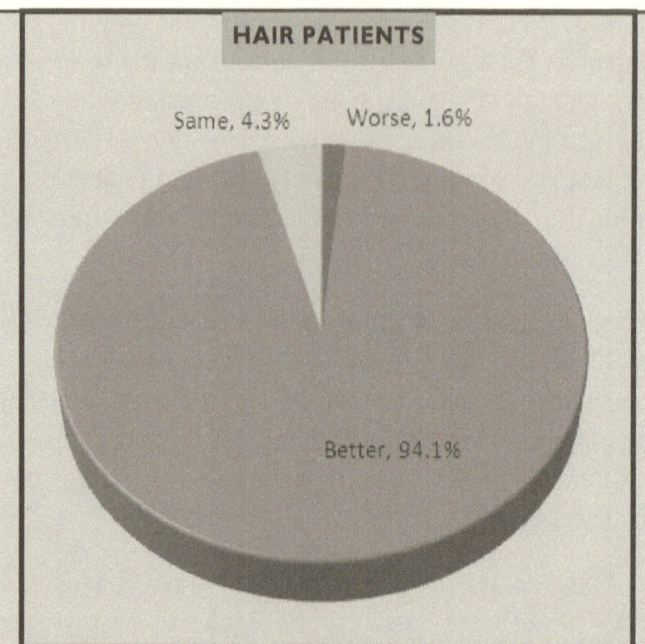

FIGURE 5: TRESS SUCCESS AT DR BATRA'S

A study conducted in-house at Dr Batra's on 1.9 lakh patients taking treatment for hair loss has shown 'improvement' in 94.1 per cent of patients; 'no change' in 4.3 per cent of patients; and, 'not better in spite of treatment' in 1.6 per cent of patients. These figures are in conformity with authenticated survey results, published by reputed external sources such as A C Nielsen and American Quality Assessors — a validation no other healthcare group in the area of hair loss treatment can show, or match.

1. "90 per cent of Dr Batra's hair patients won't change to any other Brand of treatment" — A C Nielsen Study

2. "Over 1.9 lakh hair patients treated. 94 per cent treatment satisfaction" — American Quality Assessors.

Homeopathy is different from conventional medicine, where individuals are diagnosed on the basis of just the illness or disease — and, the same medicine is given for each condition.

Homeopathy prescribes a different remedy for a given illness, depending on a multitude of factors, such as the personality of the individual, their state of mind and lifestyle. In other words, the illness may be the same by name, but the presentation of the illness in no two individuals is the same — so, they are given two different homeopathic remedies that suit their distinctive personality, or individuality.

Here are some of the commonly used homeopathic remedies for hair conditions —

Condition	Homeopathic Remedy	Indication
Male pattern baldness	Thuja Occidentalis	Strong family history of baldness
Alopecia areata	Fluoric Acid	Smooth, bald patches on the scalp. Sudden hair loss after fever
Dandruff	Kali Sulphuricum	Thick dandruff. Dry scalp, intense itching followed by burning
Psoriasis of scalp	Mezereum	Psoriatic patches on scalp with intense itching and hair loss
Hair loss, after delivery	Sepia	Hair falls out in large numbers after delivery
Drug-induced hair loss	Nux Vomica	Hair loss from taking allopathic drugs, or after chemotherapy
Hair that is dry, brittle	Psorinum	Lustreless, dry, rough hair. There may be humid eruptions on the scalp
Hair loss from stress	Natrum Muriaticum	Prolonged stress, or grief that leads to chronic hair loss
Menopausal hair loss	Lachesis	Hot flashes, mood swings
Jaundice	Chelidonium	Dry hair, falling of hair from the back of the head.

Remember!

Important: Speak to your homeopath, as regards appropriate dosage/s and duration of treatment. Please do not self-treat, or self-medicate.

WIGS

A useful non-surgical hair replacement system, wigs can be a good answer for temporary hair loss, or in conditions where medical or surgical treatment cannot offer long-lasting solutions.

 Wigs can be useful in people who have —

🪮 Pattern hair loss in men, Stage 6 and 7; Grade 3 in women

🪮 Patchy hair loss (alopecia areata), with large patches

🪮 Alopecia totalis

🪮 Alopecia universalis

🪮 Patchy scarring hair loss

🪮 Trichotillomania — large patches.

The wig is an 'advanced' version of the practice of using toupees to cover hair loss, which goes back to the beginning of time. It is a different thing that they are a butt of jokes — right from slapstick clips to cartoons — or, of one's toupee or wig flying away — for just as long.

A toupee is a small piece of hair. It can be made of real, or synthetic, hair. It is essentially a mesh or fabric foundation worn around to camouflage or 'cover' a bald patch, or thinning hair area on the scalp.

Wigs are improved or refined 'cousins' of the toupee. They cover more 'surface' area than toupees. They are known by different names — hairpieces, rugs, hair units or hair systems. Modern wigs are an advance. They are almost undetectable — they are so well anchored that no gusty wind can blow them off. Well, almost.

There are speciality shops for wigs, not to speak of online stores. The market for wigs has rapidly expanded so that it is today nothing short of a billion dollar industry.

Remember, a wig is quite expensive. It needs to be replaced once a year, or once in two years — subject to its quality and durability. You should also, perhaps, have a back-up, like you have for your electronic data. It's advisable to have a spare wig — like a spare handkerchief.

TYPES OF WIGS

Machine-made wigs are a cheaper option. Although they appear realistic, they lose their appeal when the wind blows — once this happens, the netting below (used to 'fix' it in place) gets noticeable and evident. These wigs are not certainly part of your full-fledged hair replacement system.

Hand-made wigs have a realistic feel and appeal. The reason for this is that each strand of hair is sewn individually — not as strips

HAIR-FILE

Indian hair is apparently a wig's 'best bet and friend.'

Why? Because it is thicker and usually longer than European hair. Hence, it makes for good wigs.

Most of the hair, for Indian wigs, come from a famous temple-town in South India—a billion-rupee-plus export industry. While millions of devotees flock and 'tonsure' their hair, to fulfil a vow, or ritual, what they may not know is their hair is sold to make wigs.

Indian hair has a natural look and feel. It has been used, for ages, by workmen and manufacturers, who make better quality human hair wigs.

The best part: Indian hair, unlike European or Asian hair, does not need extra 'processing.' It also has more body and, therefore, is a better choice for making wigs.

Besides, Indian hair is less expensive. It is, therefore, a preferred choice — not because of its instant appeal and value for money, for everyone, but also because it meets the need for a more silky textured human hair wig, for the sophisticated.

— to make the hair move more naturally. The best part is — you can order a custom-made, or personalised, wig. In other words, you can sport hand-made wigs as you style your own hair.

The price for good, quality wigs start at around Rs 1 lakh. They require regular maintenance.

Most modern wigs are made from wefts of hair or synthetic fibre. A weft is a ribbon or string of hair which is sewn closely together in strands. They may be machine sewn, or handmade.

WEAVE-EXTENSION

Some people refer to a weave as a hair system; it is more of an attachment. A weave involves a wig on a mesh foundation, where strands of your natural hair are woven through the edges of the foundation to secure the weave. The 'woven' attachment 'holds the hair system to your scalp firmly and naturally because of its many points of attachment.

Hair extensions are nowadays used to achieve volume, colour and length. If you are in-between transition from growing out hair, they are perfect as you can avoid having to wait. Your hair will grow. Besides, if you have fine hair or hair that does not grow, hair extensions can be used to achieve instant volume or length. The downside is itching, pull on hair and, of course, losing it!

Standard or Wefted

This is the most common form of wigs. It has a standard or wefted cap.

The wig has a permatease which is a 'crimping effect' done at the root of the wig to create a permanent volumised look. The permatease allows you to move the style around from side-to-side and offers flexibility.

One variant of the standard cap is the 'capless' wig. Instead of a lace top, the wefted hair/fibre is continued over the top (crown) of the head.

The advantage of this wig is it is lightweight and 'cooler' to wear, with the wefts well 'spaced out' than the normal wig spacing. The disadvantage is it has less coverage with a smaller amount of fibres. This can present a 'quirk' with your own hair showing through. This type of wig may not be the ideal type, if you want to cover your own scalp!

Monofilament Wigs

Monofilament wigs — or, new-generation wigs — refer to nylon or polyester micromesh into which individual hair strands are 'fixed' with hand. This gives the chimera-effect of skin by revealing the wearer's scalp colour through the mesh. The monofilament wig provides the most flexible and natural-looking style, as the hair can be brushed and parted in any which way you may like.

The material is more soft than the standard wig — it is most useful for those who have sensitive scalps or total hair loss.

The Style Option

It's not easy as you'd think to choose a new hairstyle wig. It is up to you, or your stylist, to evaluate and consider a hairstyle that suits your profile.

You'd also decide whether to go radical or gradually change or increase your hair and buy several wigs, each one a little different, so that no one would notice.

- Choose a wig in the same manner you choose a hairstyle

- Make sure it is as unique as your signature or fingerprint

- Make sure too that it suits your skin tone and your facial contour.

Consult or speak to your trichologist. This can help you find the right style of wig and weave.

Attaching a Wig

Glue. Glue around the outer edge of the hair system holds the wig in place

Clips. These are attached to your hair system and surrounding fringe of normal hair

Double-sided Tape. This is attached to your hair system. You 'stick it' to your shaved scalp.

Weave. The weave is a different thing. It sews hair that you have into the foundation mesh. The hair anchors the hair system to your scalp. However, when hair continues to grow, the hair system gets loose over time. Most weaves need to be tightened every week (*Note:* Traction alopecia can result from long-term use of weaves).

Wig Advantage

◊ Fast and easy result (within a few hours) without a surgical procedure.

Disadvantages

♀ A rapid change in appearance when the hair system is first used

♀ Lack of durability

♀ Frequent cleaning and repairs

♀ You need to have a back-up plan — or, 'duplicate' when one is 'under repair'

♀ Somewhat unnatural frontal hairline

- Disagreeable smell from scalp sebum (natural oil) build-up

- Speedy hair loss caused by the hair system

- Problem of rejection in certain cases.

Although you just can't argue, while replacing, repairing, washing or otherwise fooling around with wigs, they can be more expensive than having a hair transplant, albeit the initial cost is low. However, many people opt for wigs, instead of transplants, accepting the long-term costs. After years or so, or when a person ages to a point where pride isn't such a big issue, he or she can decide it's time to go natural with a hair transplant.

There's also fear among wig users that wigs are too obvious and clumsy. Although there's no such thing as a completely detection-free and worry-free wig system, high quality wigs can look quite real. Apart from being expensive, they require careful and constant maintenance.

ONE FLEW THRO' THE WIG'S NEST

Varoon played cricket at the state level. No one knew that, at age 25, Varoon had a wig attached with glue. His batting partner once played a ball gently into a vacant area and called for a run. Varoon responded. A fielder suddenly appeared from nowhere — Varoon had to run for his life! In his attempt to 'beat the throw,' he slipped and fell in one heap. The result — his wig fell far behind him, exposing the front of his clean-shaven bald head, where the glue 'resided.' The small crowd roared with glee — at his expense. Varoon's 'best guarded' hair secret was out! The flying wig is the most terrifying 'nightmare-come-true' — more so, when the attachment moves, because of loose, uncut inner hair. Sometimes, the bonding system, like Varoon's wig, can get loose. One simple trick that can help avoid such a 'nightmarish' experience is to pay close attention to the wig, keeping the bonding tape or glue secure and attending to hair growth below the hair system from time to time.

Ah, Not that Fetid Smell Again

Bad smell is yet another terrifying prospect for wig users. The reason being bacteria can grow on exfoliated skin, while sebum builds up under hair replacement systems. Maintaining hygiene is, therefore, not easy.

One simple idea that works is to wash your hair system regularly. It is always better to own two wigs, and use them alternatively. This ensures their dryness and hygiene.

Yes, there are problems with the 'hygiene premise' too. Washing wigs too frequently is going to ruin the wig, unless you take great care while cleaning and drying them.

One well-kept 'secret' is splashing cologne on your wig before wearing it.

HAIR CONCEALERS

Arvind came to me with a forlorn, anxious look. He said he was getting married in the next few days. He was endlessly worried about a bald patch on his scalp. He said he'd won a bride, all right, but would he be able to win over his 'hair loss' battle?

We counselled him and told him that the 'breach' could be fixed with a handy 'quick-fix.' We also told him that it (fibre concealer) would sure mask his 'lack of full hair' in areas that 'mattered,' naturally — so much so, that nobody would get to know of it. He appeared to be somewhat relieved.

We now impressed upon him the fact that it would be ideal for him to take medical treatment, because concealers only 'hide' bald spots. They don't treat hair loss. We told him that his hair loss was moderate and the prospect of benefit from medical treatment was bright for him. He returned to us a few weeks after his marriage and honeymoon, to opt for medical treatment. The treatment paid off; Arvind now sports healthy hair.

He says, with a beaming smile, "I'm so grateful for your 'prompt' quick-fix, which worked wonders, followed by professional medical treatment. It has been like hair today, hair tomorrow for me. Your medical treatment and advice has not only changed my life, it has also helped me overcome my lurking fear of going bald like some of my friends."

Hair concealers play an obvious role — they conceal, or camouflage, hair loss. However, a lot depends on how they are applied, used and what results you'd expect in practical terms. Primarily, because hair concealers are keyed to provide cosmetically supportive, or adjuvant 'cover,' in hair loss for many people — especially those who are beginning to witness hair loss. Nothing more.

The fundamental advantage is — there is no surgery involved, the cost is minimal and results are instant. In other words, when the concealers' particulates are 'sprinkled' on hair, the results are perceptible in a jiffy.

One popular brand is Toppik. It has organic keratin fibres similar to those found in human hair. The fibres adhere to hair through static electricity, so thinning areas appear thicker and fuller — instantly.

It just takes a few seconds to apply the fibre concealer, such as Toppik, and feel great.

Spray-on Hair Concealers

Spray-on concealers are also quick and easy-to-use. They darken the scalp, filling in thin areas by creating the impression of greater area coverage.

All you need to do is hold the spray-can eight inches away from your head and spray in an even pattern. The tiny fibres that match with your hair colour will naturally stick to your hair and darken your scalp.

Advantage

- ♦ Quick and easy-to-use

- ♦ They provide instantaneous results

- ♦ Look natural

Disadvantage

Hair concealers provide immediate results, but they come with their own 'riders' —

- ♀ They can get washed off, if you are out in the rain

- ♀ Lead to dependence; you may not want to step out without having them on

- Spray concealers may not work on the hairline, if you have a receding hairline

- Sometimes the application may be untidy

- They do not work when one is completely bald. They need at least some hair to hold on

- They do not treat hair loss; they merely hide it

- Stain light-coloured clothes; hence, can be a reason for embarrassment.

If you are looking for permanent treatment for your hair loss, hair concealers are not for you.

They may fill the role of a temporary 'quick-fix' as you await another treatment, provided your expectations are realistic, not fanciful.

Most important: any which way you look at it, concealers or no concealers, you will need medical treatment to treat, stop or control hair loss.

HAIR FOUNDATION

Call it just an aesthetic 'quick-fix,' yet foundations come in handy when you want to hide that tiny bald patch that is visible on the scalp.

Much like a foundation that women use on their face during a make-up, hair foundations are meant for application on the scalp. You must pick a colour that matches your hair colour. The foundation can be applied with a brush, or sponge.

Advantages

- Masks hair thinning promptly

- Easy-to-use

Disadvantages

- Only conceals areas of hair thinning–not bigger bald patches on the scalp

- Can't be used on the hair line

- Don't add fullness or volume to your hair (like fibres)

- Has to be re-applied after every hair wash.

LASER THERAPY

LASER THERAPY

The term 'Laser treatment' may flash a thought about hair removal in your mind, but the fact is lasers can also be used for hair growth.

Low Level Laser Therapy (LLLT), or laser photo-therapy, or LaserComb, is a new medical approach. It is a non-invasive, painless treatment option for treating hair loss.

LLLT does not produce heat. It can be used to heal damaged tissues. It decreases inflammation. It increases the blood flow and oxygen supply to the root of the hair and scalp, thus stimulating hair growth.

It also brings about a nutrient-rich environment to the hair follicle, while promoting healthier natural hair overall. It is effective for both men and women. However, you need to continue with regular usage of Low Level Laser Therapy for sustained results.

LASER WORKS

The LaserComb works on the scientific principle of 'photo-biostimulation' and progressively improves the appearance of your hair.

Remember! There are approximately 3,500 positive scientific studies of Low Level Laser Therapy published internationally. In 2003, an independent report by the Hair and Scalp Clinic, Florida, US, verified the correlation between LaserComb use and positive benefits to hair.

The LaserComb harnesses the energising and nourishing effects of photo-therapy, to make hair look healthy and vibrant. Light is energy. Living cells thrive with light and your hair is no exception.

The end result is the appearance of your hair in 'better light' — as it flourishes, you will feel good and happy about your hair again.

Handheld Laser for Home Use

Hand-held laser devices, such as brushes and combs, that emit Low Laser Light, are said to stimulate hair growth and make you look more youthful.

They are quite handy. The device is held at the front of the hairline and slowly moved backwards towards the crown at 4-second intervals. This is repeated in the opposite direction.

For best results, the technique needs to be performed for 15 minutes, three times a week.

Results are conflicting and opinion is divided among experts and users alike. However, no safety issues have been reported.

HAIR TRANSPLANTATION

Baldness, especially in men, is perceived as a sign of old age, lack of appeal, and infertility.

Although none of these signs may be true, clinical studies have shown that hair loss is a cause of low self-esteem and low self-confidence in men.

Over 75 per cent of men and 50 per cent of women experience some degree of hair loss in their lifetime. Causes of hair loss, as you would already know, emerge from a host of factors, but primarily from genes, hormones and age.

Men, in the past, often restored to frantic measures in trying to conceal their hair loss — most often with disastrous outcomes.

Hair treatment and restoration have vastly improved in recent years. Among the many options used for hair restoration, hair transplantation is being hailed as the most effective treatment for baldness. For all the right reasons.

Hair transplantation is an office surgical procedure — it simply relocates existing hair follicles from the donor site on the back of the scalp to the balding area.

The procedure first begins with the surgeon identifying

NOT JUST THE HEAD!

Having pubic hair is a trend in South Korea, where it is regarded as a sign of fertility. Besides, Korean men of all ages consider it inauspicious to have sexual relationship with a woman without pubic hair. No wonder many Korean women were paying as much as £1,700 (about Rs 1,30,000) to have hair transplanted from their heads to their pubic region!

The structure of head and pubic hair in Asians is fairly similar. The implanted hair is not long; it seldom falls out.

a donor strip from the donor site — this, as you know, is often located on the back, or sides of the scalp.

During the procedure, local anaesthesia is administered to relieve any uneasiness.

Your surgeon will first remove a strip of skin from the donor area and close the opening with self-absorbable sutures. Remember, this is painless and you don't feel a thing.

The donor strip is, thereafter, cut into three sizes of grafts — the micrograft, the single follicular unit, and the modified follicular unit. The single follicular unit has about two and the modified follicular unit has 2-4 hairs.

Once this is done, the surgeon and surgical team segregate individual hair follicles from the donor strip and implant them to the balding region.

The grafts are inserted into your balding areas and tactically intended to aesthetically improve the volume of your existing hair, reconstruct the hairline and fill in balding areas.

The whole procedure takes just about 3-5 hours, depending on the number of grafts.

Hair transplantation has a high success rate as long as you have enough donor hair. The side-effects, if any, are minimal, as are potential complications, such as infection and swelling.

There is often a fine scar on the donor area which is camouflaged with the surrounding hair. You will feel minimal or no pain. The best part is you can return to work the next day.

Yet another big advantage is there is no additional care needed for the transplanted hair. You may treat it like your normal, ordinary hair.

No need to guess why — it is your own hair.

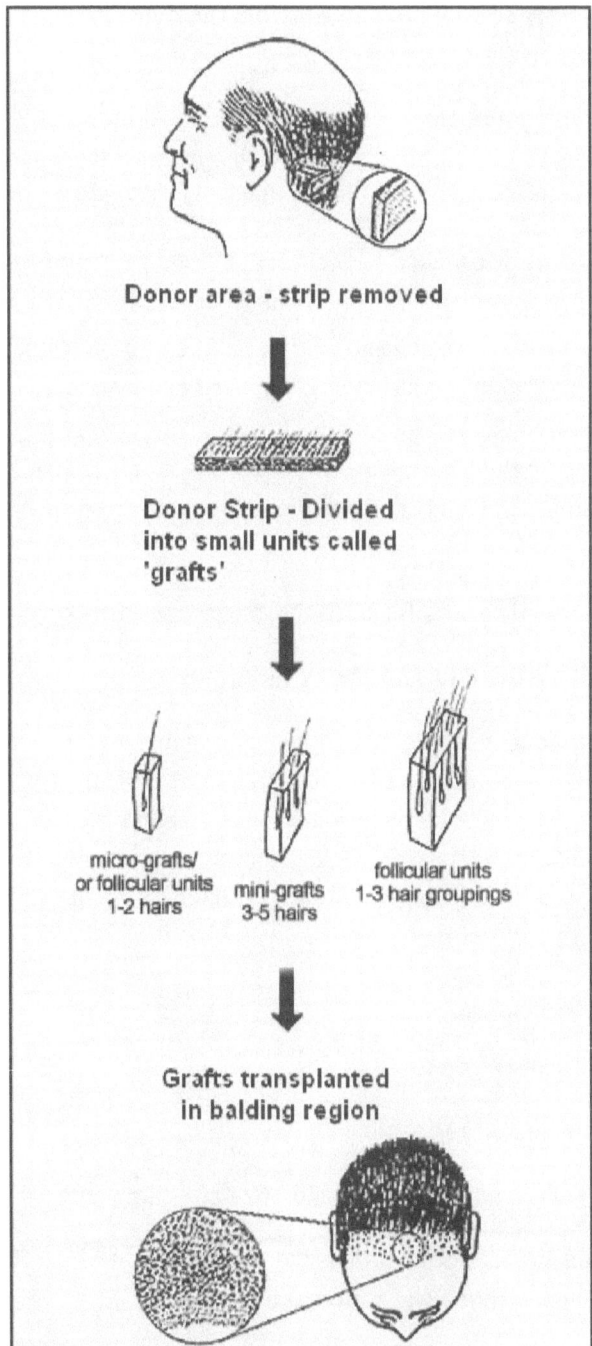

Donor area - strip removed

Donor Strip - Divided into small units called 'grafts'

micro-grafts/
or follicular units
1-2 hairs

mini-grafts
3-5 hairs

follicular units
1-3 hair groupings

Grafts transplanted in balding region

FIGURE 6: HAIR TRANSPLANTATION: STEP-BY-STEP

It is currently possible to harvest from the donor area, up to 5,000 hair in a single session.

The transplanted hair will start to grow in 4-6 months. It will have the same strength, colour, texture, length and life span as your 'normal' hair derived from your donor area.

There are two primary techniques in which donor grafts are extracted and implanted in the bald areas, viz., —

1. *Follicular Unit Extraction* (FUE) is a hair harvesting method of hair transplantation in which hair is removed one-by-one from the donor area.

2. *Follicular Unit Transplantation* (FUT) is a hair transplantation technique in which a 'strip' of hair is removed from the donor area.

Note: The final results for both the procedures are the same

FOLLICULAR UNIT EXTRACTION (FUE)

This technique has evolved into a minimally invasive technique, just like the evolution of brain, heart, joints, prostate and intestinal surgeries in which conventional incisions are no longer used. Follicular unit extraction (FUE) allows the surgeon to remove individual follicular units without making a donor incision, or removing a strip of donor scalp.

Advantages

◊ No scar in the donor area

◊ Relatively quicker healing

◊ Minimal discomfort in the donor area after the grafts are removed

◊ All routine exercise, sports and fitness activities can be resumed within a week after the procedure.

◊ Better for smaller sessions.

FOLLICULAR UNIT TRANSPLANTATION (FUT)

Follicular unit transplantation (FUT) was a major advance in hair restoration since hair transplants were first introduced in the US in the late 1950s.

Hair is removed from the permanent zone (from the back and sides of the scalp) in a linear strip and transplanted into areas affected by balding, using only naturally occurring, individual follicular units.

Advantages

☼ Can get more hair per session

☼ Multiple sessions become easier

☼ Better results because of more hair

☼ Cheaper than FUE

☼ Less time consuming.

Who's A Good Candidate for Hair Transplant Surgery...

Most people feel comfortable with a medical option. Not so

HAIR-FILE

Hair is genetically programmed to grow, stay and then shed. Thinning and balding occur when hair follicles are susceptible to DHT (the hormone that destroys hair follicles). As a result, shedding of hair exceeds new growth.

Hair, located in a horse-shoe shaped pattern at the back of the head (donor area), is generally resistant to DHT. It is also genetically programmed to grow for the rest of your life. Hair transplantation is the process of removing a small section of hair from the donor area and inserting it into the thinning and balding area.

Hair transplantation is a pain-free, office-based procedure, performed under local anaesthesia. The individual is conscious and comfortable during the procedure and can watch TV, talk, make phone calls, or just relax. They can go home immediately, following the procedure, and get back to work in a day or two. The transplanted hair can be groomed, shampooed and combed in any style you like.

with surgery, howsoever safe and simple it may be.

The first question before anyone opts for the procedure is: "Do I really need a hair transplant?" This is not a simple, straightforward question.

Let me put it in perspective. Hair transplantation should not be anyone's first treatment of choice when one starts to lose hair. Besides, not everyone who's balding is a good candidate for hair transplantation. Let's 'zero-in' on the 'right' or 'best' candidates for a hair transplant. This will include individuals who have —

☑ Male pattern baldness

☑ Enough donor hair to supply balding areas

☑ Good general health.

... And, Who is Not

☒ Most women — because they often have thin hair all over the scalp, including the sides and back. However, hair transplantation can benefit women who have lost some, but not all hair — from causes such as burns, or other scarring trauma or injury to the scalp, eyebrows or eyelashes and some cases of pattern hair loss

☒ Men with diffuse alopecia, who have an unhealthy donor supply

☒ People with low hair densities, or less donor hair

☒ Individuals with a tight or inelastic scalp

☒ Patchy hair loss.

Ideally, men under 25 years of age should think twice before they undergo a transplant procedure, while 'distilling' the following pointers:

- Have I examined other options and discussed them with my trichologist?

- Does my hair loss really trouble me?

- Have I given medical treatment a good try and waited long enough for results to emerge?

It is imperative for the emotionally distressed hair loss individual to make informed choices and understand the long-term implications of any treatment option — especially hair transplantation procedure — in consultation with a professional trichologist.

Remember, a good decision made today should emerge as a wise, well-informed and well-chosen decision tomorrow.

ADVANTAGES OF HAIR TRANSPLANTATION

- Natural and permanent solution to hair thinning and baldness
- You get your own natural hair growing back for the rest of your life
- Hair can be combed, oiled, washed, cut and styled the way you want
- Day-care procedure — you can go home the same day after procedure
- You can resume work from the next day itself — no prolonged leave from work is required
- Natural appearance at every stage of the process
- Great results giving you aesthetic, youthful look
- No on-going maintenance is necessary
- Does away with wigs or hair concealers!
- Ditch the comb over!

In addition —

▶ Studies on the emotional or psychological impact of balding report a definitive psycho-emotional improvement after hair transplant surgery

▶ Greater patient satisfaction, improved self-esteem and self-confidence

▶ Greater positive impact on sex life and job performance and career in people who had less hair loss at the time of transplant compared to those who had more advanced stages of hair loss — although you will have to continue taking medical treatment.

It goes without saying that individuals who suffer the most from hair loss are the most likely to benefit psychosocially, although realistic expectations are just as important before undergoing a surgical hair restoration procedure.

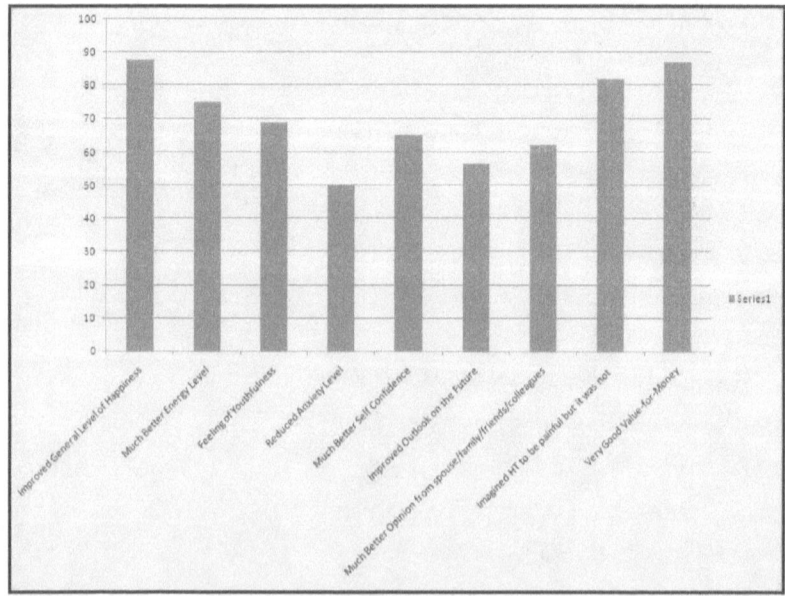

FIGURE 7: RESULTS OF DR BATRA'S SURVEY ON EMOTIONAL BENEFITS OF HAIR TRANSPLANT

WHY WE LAUNCHED Dr BATRA'S B PERFECT

We started Dr Batra's B Perfect, because we always thought that if we'd only standardise hair transplants in India, there would be no need for hair transplant patients to go abroad and shell out hefty fees for the same procedure. Besides, we'd bring down expenses, while adding the Indian healing touch. More than anything else, we felt that an initiative, such as Dr Batra's B Perfect Aesthetic Clinics, would meet the needs of patients who were looking for world-class, and yet less expensive option.

Highlights

1. Standardised

2. Available all over India

3. Not priced exorbitantly; hence, affordable to all

4. No need to fly abroad

5. We've brought the best for you in India

6. Team of highly-specialised, well-trained and technologically-advanced plastic surgeons

CHOOSING THE SURGEON

Hair transplant is not just an art, but also a dexterous science. A good surgeon can 'sculpt' a symmetrical and 'natural' reconstruction of hair line and achieve the illusion of fullness — even when the need for hair follicles exceeds the supply. For instance, it's not uncommon for the hair restoration surgeon to restore just one area of the bald scalp in an extremely bald person. The reason being, putting hair in the front and leaving the crown thin or bald creates a natural-looking variation of a typical balding man who has only top balding. When you view from the front, the hair looks normal; whereas from the back, the balding crown is visible.

In other words, the most important factor for hair transplant is choosing the right surgeon. Opt for a surgeon who has the best credentials — with a statistical 'roll-call' of a large number of successful hair transplants.

Precautions

Your hair transplant surgeon will order an electrocardiogram (ECG), blood coagulation, blood sugar, HIV, and hepatitis B and C tests, a few days before surgery — to ascertain or rule out certain health issues or concerns.

Your surgeon will also advice you to avoid the use of anti-inflammatory drugs, including non-steroidal anti-inflammatory drugs (NSAIDs; e.g., nimesulide), or aspirin, a week before hair transplant procedure, as also vitamin E supplements, 2-3 weeks before procedure. The 'duo' can cause excess bleeding after procedure.

Individuals who are anxious are given a sedative before procedure. This helps them to relax.

Antibiotics are often prescribed a day before surgery and continued for 4-7 days, subject to the hair transplant surgeon's view.

A CASE IN POINT

Rajeev (28) started losing hair in his early twenties. He looked older than his age due to his receding hairline. Being a marketing professional, looking smart and young was important for him. He was disturbed, because prospective brides did not 'approve' of him. This was turning out to be too upsetting — it 'stumped' his self-confidence. His parental pressure to marry was also driving him to his wit's end. He decided to give hair transplantation a 'go.'

His hair transplant was done in one sitting; it was painless. He was absolutely fit after the procedure. He resumed work a day or two later. It has been 12 months since the procedure and Rajeev now has a head full of natural, growing hair that is permanent.

Rajeev is a different person today — no longer gloomy. He is full of confidence and happily engaged, Says Rajeev, "I was initially reluctant to consider this option. On the persistence and coaxing of my mother, I hesitantly underwent the procedure. But, when I look at my head now (12 months after procedure), I have to say that it was completely worth it. I would recommend the procedure to anyone wanting to replace baldness with natural looking hair."

HAIR LOSS SOLUTIONS:
A STUDY IN COMPARISON

	Medical Treatment	Wig, Toupee, Hairpiece	Hair Transplant
Permanent results	X	X	√
Natural results	√	X	√
No maintenance required	X	X	√
Safe for existing hair	√	X	√
One-time cost	X	X	√
No after-care worries	√	X	√
Good for large areas of baldness	X	√	X

Hair Transplant: FUT & FUE: What to Expect?

	Strip Method (Follicular Unit Transplantation)	FUE (Follicular Unit Extraction)
Scar	Linear	Multiple pinpoint scars
Visibility of scars	No (Unless head is shaved bald)	No
Number of hair transplanted	More	Comparatively less
Multiple sessions	Can be done	Less likely
Procedure time	Comparatively less	Comparatively more
Cost to patient	Comparatively less	Comparatively more
Area covered	Better for large sessions (more hair)	Better for small sessions (less hair)

QUESTIONS YOU ALWAYS WANTED TO ASK ABOUT HAIR TRANSPLANTS BUT NEVER DID

1. What Is Hair Transplantation?

Hair transplantation is a procedure in which hair is picked from the back of the scalp — where even bald men never lose hair — and, transplanted in the balding area.

Thus, you get:

- Completely natural, growing hair

- Permanent hair

- An aesthetically pleasing, youthful look.

2. Are the Results Permanent?

- Yes, the results of hair transplantation are permanent

- Hair from the back of the scalp is genetically programmed to grow for the rest of your life

- It grows permanently even when transplanted in the balding region.

3. Is Special Maintenance Required?

- The transplanted hair requires no special maintenance

- It can be treated just like normal hair

- The hair can be washed, combed, oiled, cut and styled normally giving natural and excellent aesthetic results.

4. **Is Hair Transplantation Painful?**

- Hair transplantation is not painful

- It is so comfortable that while the procedure is going on, you can watch TV, read a book or chat with your friends on your mobile phone.

5. **Is Hair Transplantation Safe?**

- Hair transplantation is absolutely safe; it has no side effects

- As a precautionary measure though, a series of tests are done before the procedure to ensure that you are fit for undergoing surgery.

6. **How Soon Can I Get Back to Work?**

- You can resume work on the next day after hair transplantation, though surgeons often recommend that you take a break for a day before resuming work

- No hassles of taking long leave from your work. This adds to the convenience of the procedure.

7. **Who Is an Ideal Candidate for Hair Transplant?**

- Men who are losing hair from top and frontal portion of the head (male pattern baldness) are ideal candidates

- Women suffering from hair loss can also benefit from hair transplantation

- Age is no constraint — anyone from 21 years right up to 80 years can go for hair transplant.

8. When Can I See Results after Hair Transplantation?

- The newly transplanted hair is visible even on the day of the procedure

- The hair starts growing gradually and you can notice the steady difference month after month.

- For hair to grow to your normal full length and observe the full result of the procedure, it may take around 9-12 months.

9. Do I Have to Continue Medicines Even after a Hair Transplant?

The transplanted hair does not need treatment, but it is advisable that you continue medication after the procedure so that your natural hair doesn't fall out. Preventing hair loss from the rest of your scalp is also important — to get the 'best look' post-transplantation.

10. Is It Necessary to Shave Hair Before Hair Transplantation?

No, it is not necessary to shave hair before hair transplantation. The only exception is a large session of FUE — for which only the back of the head may require a 'shave.'

Top Tips

TOP 10 TIPS: DOS AND DONT'S

1. Take 1-2 days off from work and rest well after your procedure

2. Do NOT drink alcohol for 48 hours following your procedure. Alcohol thins the blood and may cause bleeding

3. Do NOT take aspirin for 3 days after procedure as it can thin the blood

4. Eat and then take your medications as soon as possible after your transplant procedure

5. Wear protection on your head — when outside in sunlight or rain, for the first 10 days after the transplant

6. Lie down and rest for 2-3 hours after procedure. When sleeping or resting, lie flat on your back with two pillows under your head

7. Limit all strenuous activities for two weeks after the procedure — this includes dancing, jogging, diving, lifting heavy objects and especially vigorous work-outs. You can walk briskly, swim or play golf after 5-7 days. You can have sex after 24 hours

8. Do not comb your hair on the day of the transplant. On the day following your transplant, you may gently comb your hair. Avoid scraping the scalp with your comb

9. Be cautious when applying moisturiser, gel, serum, hair oil, conditioner or hair spray, as they can cause discomfort. Resume your normal hair care routine 3 weeks after procedure, or once all scabs are gone

10. Cut, dye and shower — It is advised not to cut or colour the hair for at least 3-4 weeks after procedure. Also, avoid direct shower for at least 1 week after the procedure. Use a mug instead.

OF CLONING, GENES & STEM CELL THERAPY

Modern hair transplants provide excellent treatment results, yet they are not without certain limitations.

Remember, you can get as much hair for a transplant, subject to the hair available in donor areas — that is, on the back of the head. Larger bald areas cannot be covered completely with a hair transplant.

Besides, the older you get, or the more 'balder' you get, you will need to cover larger bald areas with diminishing amounts of donor hair.

The obvious question, therefore, is: "What if I can clone my hair, or, have my own hair replicated in the laboratory, so that it will produce as many hair as I want, or need, for hair transplant?"

'Cloning' or hair follicle re-engineering is one such idea which can fill that hope, even if it is not as simple as it appears to be.

This is because there is more to 'hair' than meets the scalp.

It all began when Dr Colin Jahoda, a British scientist, took hair cells from his own scalp and transplanted them into his wife's forearm. The cells encouraged new hair growth on his wife's arm.

Hair cells have been found to 'stir up' new hair growth without having to transplant the whole hair follicle.

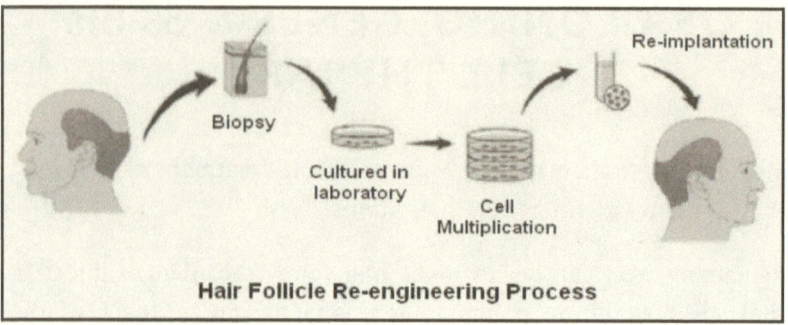

Hair Follicle Re-engineering Process

FIGURE 8: CLONING: STEP-BY-STEP

The technical 'impasse' with the cloning advance, at the moment, is —

▶ The ability to clone hair cells has to be replicated and proven

▶ The cells will have to grow in the right direction on the scalp, not under the skin or downward

▶ It is not yet fully established whether 'cloned' follicles will continue to grow hair after the initial hair growth is shed (in cycles of 2-6 years, like normal follicles)

▶ It is not yet known whether the 'cloned' cells have any side effects.

Scientists are working at a frenetic, exciting pace, to find practical answers to the dilemma. It is just a question of time, therefore, for hair cloning to become a scientific reality.

STEM CELLS

Stem cell therapy is thought to be the 'Holy Grail' of hair loss treatment.

What are stem cells? Stem cells are a class of undifferentiated cells that are able to 'differentiate' into specialised cell types. Stem cells come from two main sources:

- Embryos formed during embryological development (embryonic stem cells)

- Adult tissue (adult stem cells).

Stem cells do not serve any one function; they have the capacity to serve any function, after they are 'coached' to specialise.

Every cell in the body, for example, is derived from first few stem cells formed in the early stages of embryological development.

Stem cells extracted from embryos can, therefore, be 'coached' to become any desired cell type.

This property makes stem cells powerful enough to regenerate damaged tissue under the right conditions. This also holds exciting new possibilities in medical research and advanced, super-specialised treatment of disease, including the treatment of hair loss.

In a recent study, Japanese researchers successfully grew hair on hairless mice by implanting follicles created from stem cells, while sparking new hopes of a cure for baldness.

In another study, researchers at Yale University, US, discovered that stem cells within the skin's fatty layer were necessary to 'prompt' hair growth in mice. The insight may lead to new treatments for baldness.

Men with male pattern baldness continue to have stem cells in follicle roots, but these stem cells lose the ability to 'jump-start' hair regeneration. Scientists have known that such follicle stem cells need signals from within the skin to grow hair, but the source of such signals has been unclear, so far. It is just a question of time, again, for new stem cells breakthroughs to emerge — to treat baldness.

Stem cell has not reached clinical stages (*Source*: surgery.org). What is sold in India as stem cell is not in fact stem cell at all.

PLATELET RICH PLASMA (PRP) THERAPY

This is a relatively new protocol for hair loss treatment. The technique uses the individual's own blood as growth factor.

When our hair follicles are healthy, the growth of the hair is just as healthy. Hair follicles survive on the nutrition they get from blood supply. The therapy works this way — when platelet rich plasma (PRP) is administered in the area of damaged hair follicles, it amplifies the body's naturally-occurring healing mechanisms and stimulates the growth of hair follicles, while preventing hair loss.

COSMETIC PROCEDURES, HAIR CARE, STYLING, DIET, MYTHS, TIPS, FAQS

COSMETIC PROCEDURES ON HAIR

Everyone wants to look beautiful — to have wonderful glowing skin, shiny lustrous hair and a perfectly sculpted body.

This 'desire' to look beautiful is exactly what the entire beauty and cosmetic industry thrives on. And, when it comes to hair, there are a number of cosmetic procedures that can give you just the look you want.

Let's check out a few common examples —

BLOW DRYING

Blow dryers are hair dryers that use 'hot' and 'cold' drafts of air to dry your hair. Used along with different kinds of brushes and combs, these can be employed to style your hair in a variety of ways.

Blow dryers can be used to add volume to your hair, to set the styling products and to 'fix' your hairstyle in place.

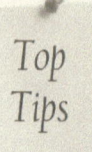

TOP 5 TIPS TO REMEMBER ABOUT THE USE OF BLOW DRYERS

1. Frequent use of a blow dryer — less than six inches from your scalp — can damage hair

2. The high heat from a blow dryer can boil the water in the hair shaft, leaving the hair brittle and 'open' to breakage

3. One trick is to allow the hair to air dry and style it after drying. This will minimise the possibility of breakage

4. It is a good practice to use a leave-in hair conditioner or hair serum before using blow dryer

5. Always end with a blast of cold air – this 'locks' in the shine and makes your hair look lustrous and gorgeous.

HAIR IRONING

Straightening irons are flat irons that use heat to straighten your hair. Curling irons or 'curling tongs,' as they are popularly known, create waves or curls in your hair using heat. Crimping irons crimp the hair in a saw-tooth fashion.

Top
Tips

TOP 5 TIPS FOR BEST RESULTS FROM HAIR IRONING

1. Your hair must be dry when you start to iron (either air dry or blow dry safely)

2. Use a good amount of leave-in hair conditioner or hair serum before using hair iron. Also your hair should be clean before your start ironing

3. Adjust the temperature — do not use very high temperature as it may cause irreparable damage to your hair

4. Go slow and take hair in small bunches to use the iron on

5. Avoid frequent use of hair iron — use it sparingly, may be only for special occasions. This will give novelty to your look for the occasion as well as prevent your hair from damage caused by frequent ironing.

BLEACHING

Hair bleaching is the use of chemicals to remove some or all of the pigment in your hair. The longer you leave the bleach mixture on hair, the greater its effect. The end result of this procedure is lightened hair that is ash or blonde-coloured.

BLEACHING DOWNSIDE

 Though it may give you a cool and a different look, bleaching is not without damaging effects. For example —

- ☞ Bleaching changes the chemistry of your hair. It opens the cuticle, or outer layer of your hair, causing hair shafts to become porous. The more porous your hair, the more dry and brittle it eventually becomes

- ☞ Global bleaching (all your scalp hair) can often give you a straw-haired look that is not appealing

- ☞ The chemicals used can cause contact allergy (dermatitis, or eczema) and chemical burns on the scalp

- ☞ Bleaching can be harmful not only to your hair and scalp, but also to your eyes.

Bleaching can have harmful effects, although a lot depends on how healthy your hair is prior to bleaching and how well you take care of it after bleaching.

Top Tips

TOP 5 TIPS FOR HAIR CARE AFTER BLEACHING YOUR HAIR

1. Choose a shampoo that has natural active ingredients on bleached hair; shampoo quickly, else it may add to the dryness of the hair

2. Condition every time you wash your hair; use leave-in hair conditioner or hair serum

3. Limit the use of styling procedures (blow drying, ironing), to avoid completely, if possible

4. Protect your hair whenever you step out in the sun (use an umbrella, hat, scarf)

5. Do not step into the pool without a swimming cap or the chlorinated water may well end up giving your bleached hair a 'green' colour.

HAIR DYEING

Hair contains natural colouring agents (called pigments) in varying proportions. That is why people have different coloured hair, such as brown, black, golden, ash, red or ginger. Loss of these pigments causes hair to turn grey. Use Dr Batra's hair dye for safe, effective and optimal results — it is free from ammonia and gives a rich colour to your hair.

Top
Tips

TOP 10 TIPS FOR HAIR DYEING/COLOURING

1. Choice of Colour. Use a hair dye which is ammonia-free, such as Dr Batra's hair dye. Also, opt for a colour that is similar to your natural colour and not drastically different

2. Patch Test. Never skip the patch skin test — it's vital to do the patch test to prevent any annoying problems later (such as allergies, scalp burns, scarring)

3. Skin Protection. Apply vaseline or petroleum jelly over your entire hairline, around your ears, etc., to prevent hair colour from getting onto your skin

4. Application. Apply the hair colour to small sections of your hair for an even application — comb with a wide-toothed comb after applying

5. Rinsing. Rinse off the dye well after keeping it for the allotted time

6. Conditioning. Condition your hair well; use a natural conditioner

7. Drying. Allow hair to air dry; avoid blow drying. This will retain the shine and lustre in your hair after colouring

8. Sun-protection. Going out in the sun for prolonged periods after colouring your hair is not advisable. Use an umbrella or hat, if you really must go out

9. Colour-Protect Shampoo. These are specifically meant for coloured hair since they are mild and help to retain colour for long

10. Washing hair rips away its natural oils. Wait for a day after hair wash so that natural oils coat your hair again. Colouring hair after this makes the dye last longer.

HAIR COLOURS

Hair colours (or, hair dyes) may be used for concealing grey hair or just to get a different look (fashion colours).

There are dozens of hair colours available in the market, largely falling into two groups — temporary or semi-permanent hair colours and permanent hair colours.

Temporary Hair Colours. These are generally ammonia-free and safer to use. They do not open up the hair shaft, but only deposit the dye into the outer layer of the hair shaft. This gets washed off bit-by-bit, with every shampoo.

Permanent Hair Colours. Largely ammonia-based, these dyes do two things — penetrate into your shaft to remove your original colour and then deposit the new colour into the shaft. The result is hair colour that lasts for a long time.

There are *natural colourants* available, such as henna and black walnut shells, besides natural bleaching agents (for lightening the hair) such as vinegar.

HAIR REBONDING

Hair rebonding is the latest hair 'buzz' among women. It is a hair straightening process which gives you super silky, great straight hair or stunning *a la* Jennifer Aniston celebrity looks, all right, but it can also make you lose a lot of hair.

What Happens in Hair Rebonding?

Hair rebonding is actually a process where the chemical bonds in your hair are broken, rearranged and bonded back again permanently using strong chemicals.

Beauty with a Price

Hair rebonding is an advertiser's dream copy, but it can be one of the most damaging things you can do to your hair. Hair is irreversibly altered after the rebonding process. In addition, chemically-treated hair shafts get weaker and fracture more easily. This can trigger

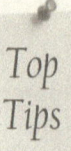

Top Tips

TOP 5 TIPS TO TAKE CARE OF HAIR THAT HAS UNDERGONE REBONDING

1. Avoid using blow dryers on rebonded hair. Avoid hot irons too, but if you must, use a hair serum generously before ironing

2. Use conditioner regularly. Oil your hair once every week

3. Do not use chemical colours on rebonded hair, as it's highly prone to chemical damage

4. Use protection when stepping out in the sun — hat, umbrella, scarf etc.

5. Trim hair regularly since split ends occur easily in chemically-treated hair and can travel quickly up the hair shaft.

hair loss. Besides, the process can also cause damage and trigger burns on the skin and scalp, if not done properly or repeated too frequently.

Hair can be damaged, if the rebonding chemicals are left on the hair for too long, or ironing is done at 180ºC.

PERMING

Perming is a cosmetic procedure that gets you 'permanent waves' in your hair. It involves the usage of chemicals that break the bonds in the hair and then re-arrange them back in order to 'fix' the waves (or, curls) in your hair.

The results of a well-done procedure are, no doubt, fabulous. It leaves you with gorgeous, curly locks that can change your appearance completely.

Perming can give you big or small curls, or even soft waves in your hair, besides adding volume to your face.

The procedure generally takes up to a few hours and the results typically last for 3-5 months.

The flipside of perming, especially after a poorly performed procedure, includes —

- Loss of elasticity of hair

- Fragile, brittle, easily breakable hair

- Hair loss even on combing gently, because hair shafts fracture easily.

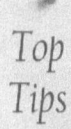

Top Tips

TOP 5 TIPS TO CARE FOR YOUR PERMED HAIR

1. Avoid colouring your permed hair — the chemicals used for perming may have already done enough damage and your hair may not be able to sustain chemicals from the colour

2. Shampoo gently — avoid aggressive hair wash

3. Be generous with the use of conditioner; use leave-in conditioner or serum

4. Towel dry or pat your wet hair gently — be careful to avoid tangles in hair

5. Avoid any hairstyle or hair accessories (rubber bands, clips, pins) that tug on your hair since this may cause hair breakage.

KERATIN THERAPY

Have you ever thought how we remember certain people associating them with typically frizzy, dry, or coarse hair — sometimes sporting a look as if the hair was a tad burnt?

A boon for all such people is keratin therapy.

Keratin is a protein that strengthens the hair shaft and protects hair from breakage.

Keratin therapy is an 'in-salon' service that infuses natural keratin deep into the hair cuticle. It is basically a smoothing system for hair. It is said to eliminate up to 95 per cent of frizz and curl — thus making hair texture smooth and shiny.

Results typically last 2-5 months, depending on your hair type. Thereafter, the procedure may have to be repeated.

TECHNIQUE

The hair is washed, dried and the keratin is combed through. The protein is ironed into the hair sections with a straightening iron. The hair becomes hard. The excess protein is washed out. Usually, the hair cannot be washed again for at least 72 hours.

The process can take 2-5 hours in the salon, where hair is ironed out in many small sections for detailed treatment.

Keratin treatment can be used for any hair type. Damaged hair soaks in more keratin; it benefits the most from the treatment.

ADVANTAGES

⚲ It reduces frizz and curl; makes hair straighter

⚲ Adds shine and silkiness to the hair; conditions the hair

⚲ Makes hair more manageable, smoother and easier to style.

DISADVANTAGE

⚲ One caveat is not to treat the hair too often, because keratin can build up, creating hard and brittle hair.

AMINEXIL TREATMENT

Aminexil is a chemical compound that was developed for treating hair loss. It is supposed to specifically control a condition in which there is premature aging of the hair follicles. The exact mechanism of how Aminexil works is not known.

Nowadays, many parlours have started giving Aminexil shots to their clients claiming that it helps to control their hair loss. The fact is hair loss needs detailed evaluation and it should be professionally treated by a trichologist — for the best results.

Aminexil shots will do no good if the cause of hair loss is internal and is left untreated. Moreover, Amenixil needs to be used regularly too.

And all said and done, as far as scientific studies are concerned, they haven't proved that Aminexil works; the drug is also not FDA-approved. On the other hand, there's no real, conclusive evidence to say that it does not work.

SHAPING YOUR HAIRSTYLE

What shape one lends to a hairstyle is a vital aesthetic element. Your hairstyle characterises your personality and lends certain uniqueness to 'you' as a person. Be it Sadhana's classic fringe, Madhuri Dixit's step-cut hair, Amitabh Bachchan's ponytailed character in *Cheeni Kum* or even the typically 'shaved' look of Amir Khan in *Ghajini* — they all make these characters unique by their hairstyle.

We strongly associate people with the way they style their hair and some of them even become the 'talk of the town' for what they do to their hair. Thus, Lasith 'Slinga' Malinga will bring to your mind the image of curly, golden locks, whereas a Christiano Ronaldo will flash the 'spiked look' through. Interestingly, David Beckham will bring you flashes of not one, but many different hairstyles.

HAIRSTYLES & CULTURE

Hairstyles are largely determined by the fashion prevalent in the culture people live in. Even in ancient times, hairstyles formed an important part of culture and traditions, all over the world.

HAIR-FILE

"If I want to knock a story off the front page, I just change my hairstyle."

– Hillary Clinton

Women would adorn their hair by braiding, stylish hair 'up-dos,' buns, chignons, colourful floral hair bands, false hair pieces, jewelled hairpins and colourful fabric accessories. Men too have adopted different hairstyles over the ages — ranging from short, cropped hair to long curls, big side-burns, while also adding accessories such as jewels and feathers.

*Top
Tips*

TOP 10 TIPS FOR SHAPING IT RIGHT

1. Your hairstyle should be in agreement with the shape of your face; it must be selected in tune with the length, shape and nature of the hair (curly, smooth, straight, or fine)

2. Don't stick to one hair parting all your life — change your parting frequently. It helps to 'jazz-up' a new look as well as prevent traction on hair due to a single, constant parting. You may experiment with zig-zag, diagonal or even curved partings

3. Comb with a thick toothed comb instead of fine comb. It helps to remove tangles easily without breaking hair. Fine-toothed comb can be used to set the final hair-do. A round or curved brush may be used to set the curls

4. Experiment with blow-dry. Set your hair in different styles using a blow dry. Do keep in mind that too much of heat can damage your hair. Use a protective serum/mousse on hair before blow drying

5. Holding gels and hair sprays may be used to secure the hairstyle in place. Men can try out different types of spikes or simply a rough-hair look using hair gels

6. If you want to add volume to your hair, bend down and back-comb your hair while using a little amount of hair spray to maintain the volume

7. If you want to get rid of the frizz, rinse your hair with a mug of cold water after shampooing and conditioning. Apply a leave-in conditioner for the hair shafts and tips

8. To flatten your wavy or curly hair, use flat iron, after applying a good amount of hair serum. Be careful not to heat the hair too much, or you'll end up damaging them

9. Clips, hairpins and scrunchies can be used to secure the style in place. Avoid using rubber bands since they tug on the hair shafts and may lead to breakage

10. Once in a while, all of us have 'bad' hair days. One of the easiest things to do is to start over. Run your hair under the tap for a quick wash and let it air dry on your way to work. If you have time, a quick blow dry will set things in place. Women may try tying up their hair in a ponytail, or bun to take care of this problem.

HAIRSTYLES TO AVOID

Certain hairstyles can cause constant tension on the hair follicle and lead to hair loss. It is best to avoid them:

☛ Cornrows

☛ Tight plaits and pigtails

☛ Pulling hair back tightly to make buns

☛ Straightening or pulling.

(NB: Also, refer to Self-Help and Chapter on Product Use for Practical Guidance).

ALL ABOUT HAIR PRODUCTS

Gone are the days when all you needed at your dressing table was some hair styling gel. Today, the market is booming with dozens of hair grooming products — and, these find a way easily onto your dressing table, sooner or later.

But, how do you choose which product is ideal for you? Whether it's supposed to be a light-hold gel or a strong-hold gel, a hair spray or a hair mousse, or how you decide when to use what? And, when should you avoid using a certain product?

Products, of course, change rapidly with fashion; they also provide a diversity of results. There may be a lot more than those covered here, but let's examine a select few.

HAIR GELS

Who has not heard about hair gels, especially when there are dozens of brands available in the market? Well, what they do is keep your hairstyle in place, make it manageable and also impart a great shine to your hair.

Gels largely belong to two categories: light-hold and strong-hold gels. As the name says it all, light-hold gels maintain the style with certain 'lightness,' whereas others give you a more 'stiff' look.

Gels are meant to be used by people with thick hair — they

HAIR-FILE

The primary reason why hair products are used is to make hair behave the way it generally does not.

Thus, straight hair can be set into curls, while curly/wavy hair can be made to fall down straight, or thick, while dense hair can be made to look 'properly set.'

give hair a wet 'set' look. Ideally, gels should not be used by people with thin hair; else, it will make them look bald.

 Some hair gels contain toxic chemicals and the alcohol content in some may make your hair dry, brittle and prone to breakage. Leaving hair gel on your hair (especially if your hair is short) may lead to grime-build up on your scalp; hence, it's a good idea to wash off the hair before the end of day.

HAIR CREAM

Hair creams help to keep hairstyle in place and prevent it from flying all over the place. They can be used when you don't want the 'stiff' or 'fixed' look that comes from using a gel. Creams also moisturise your hair, so they are good for thick, coarse hair — they also soften your look.

 Excess use of hair creams may make your hair look greasy and matted. Leaving them on the hair and scalp for long can make your scalp accumulate grime, leaving the scalp unhealthy.

HAIR POMADES

These are greasy, waxy or even water-based; they impart a slick, neat and shiny look to the user. Pomades were a rage during 1950s-1960s, with a lot of superstars opting for the pomade look.

 Wash off the pomade well at the end of day to prevent the build-up on the scalp.

HAIR WAX

These are finishing products that are similar in structure to hair pomades, though they are more petroleum-based and relatively drier. Waxes are more pliable than hair gels and can be re-styled

— they suit 'indecisive' folks, or those who need to go straight from office-look to party-look.

Waxes also give a fuller appearance to the head; hence, they are ideal for people who have thinning hair or fine hair.

 Hair wax may be difficult to wash off, so it's best to use small quantities; also, wash the head thoroughly to remove the wax; else, it will accumulate on the scalp.

HAIR LOTIONS

Lotions are aqueous solutions that contain a variety of ingredients, ranging from vitamins and moisturisers to essential oils (depending on the company that manufactures). Lotions basically rehydrate and soften dry, frizzy hair, giving your hair a smooth, silky and sexy look.

 Hair lotions may leave behind sticky and potentially unpleasant residues, when applied in excess or left on hair for long.

HAIR MOUSSE

This imparts a fuller look to hair — it is great for adding volume to fine hair. It is especially useful before getting hair curled, or set into wavy styles.

 Too much of mousse may lead to flaky residues in your hair. This is not appealing. Besides, some varieties even contain alcohol which may dry out your hair.

HAIRSTYLING FOAMS

Hair foams help to tame the frizz in the hair and come in handy to style dry, frizzy hair. They add moisture to dry hair; they also help to retain moisture and control static.

 Some of the foams contain alcohol — this may lead to dry and brittle hair, causing hair to be damaged easily.

HAIR SPRAYS

Hair sprays provide the finishing touch after styling. They are generally applied all over the head. They hold the shape of 'the' hairstyle for prolonged periods.

 Frequent use of hair sprays can make your hair brittle — this also makes hair more prone to split ends and breakage. They may dry out your scalp and give rise to dandruff too.

HAIR SERUM

Hair serums are liquids (e.g., silicone oil) that provide a nourishing, protective coat, while adding healthy moisture and gloss to the hair follicle. These are generally applied to moist hair after a hair wash.

In the process, they also fight frizz, protect hair from heat, humidity, and sun (UV) damage, or damage caused by harsh hairstyling products, perming and colouring. Hair serum, in simple terms, is a hair care solution which makes the hair glow naturally. The advantage is it does not allow hair to tangle.

 Hair serums generally contain silicones and these are water insoluble. These may build up on your scalp leading to flaky or weighed-down hair, if not washed off properly with a shampoo.

How Much Product to Use?

√ Pea-sized amount of heavier products, like a wax or pomade, is generally sufficient

√ Medium-sized amount (as much as a big coin) is good for gels, styling cream or leave-in conditioner

√ A good amount (egg-sized) is generally required for fluffy products, like a mousse.

Top Tips

TOP 10 HAIR PRODUCT TIPS

No need to wade through reams of paper for product tips. Here is a list of Top 10 product tips to help you separate the hype from the hoopla.

1. Hair colours are fun — and, always in fashion. To be a part of the fun, yet keep your hair safe, choose ammonia-free hair colours

2. Choose a shampoo that has natural active ingredients to keep your chemically-processed hair safe

3. Some hair products, such as bleach may cause irreparable damage to your hair and leave them with a 'straw-like' look — these are best avoided

4. A good hair conditioner is an integral part of a healthy hair regime. You may also opt for leave-in hair conditioner or hair serum

5. Conditioners are great, but never apply the conditioner onto your scalp — it is meant only for the hair shafts. Application on the scalp may lead to build-up of grime and make you itchy

6. Hair gels, hair creams, waxes, mousse and other styling products should preferably be washed off the same day, especially if they have come in contact with your scalp

7. Hair products, no matter how safe they are, must always be tested on your scalp — every time — before use. A patch test (using one small patch of your hair) is mandatory. Apply a small quantity of the product on a small patch of your skin, preferably behind ears, or nape of neck, or inner side of the elbow. Wait for 15 minutes and then wash off. Watch for signs of inflammation or allergy, such as redness, itching or rash.

8. Too much is never good — this is especially true for hair products. So, it's best you savour the natural look as much as possible

9. Avoid hair products that are harsh on your scalp and hair; choose natural products

10. Avoid too much of experimentation with hair products — stick to the brands that suit you well and go along.

DIET: FEEDING YOUR HAIR RIGHT

You are what you eat.

As one of the fastest growing tissues in the body, hair requires adequate nutrition for proper growth. If it does not receive adequate supply of proteins, vitamins and other essential minerals and nutrients, the result is clearly evident — hair loss and dull, dry, lustreless hair.

Hair Loss in a Diet-Crazy World

Losing weight by crash dieting and getting to 'size-zero' is a fad in these times. However, it is not without a downside — nutritional imbalance in the body. This usually shows up in the form of hair loss within 2-3 months of getting onto such 'fancy' weight loss diets.

Remember! Many young guys and girls consult me for hair loss treatment and during case-taking, they proudly claim to have lost a good amount of weight recently. What they don't understand is while it's important to have ideal weight and healthy body, one can also maintain 'normal' weight sensibly, without going on 'crash-diets.' Crash-diets only deplete the body of the necessary nutrients; the result is hair loss (and other health) problems.

Role of Proper Nutrition

Hair loss occurs when your diet is insufficient in B-vitamins, especially B5 (pantothenic acid, B3 (niacin), B6 (pyridoxine), biotin, inositol and folic acid and minerals such as magnesium, copper and zinc. B-vitamins are especially important for hair growth.

Essential amino acids (that come from proteins) are just as important. They are known to control thinning and thickening of hair.

Essential fatty acids perk up hair texture, while preventing dry, brittle hair. A deficiency in essential fatty acids may lead to hair dryness, change of hair colour, redness of the scalp and flaking.

However, too much of a good thing can be bad too. Eating large plates of vitamin A (such as 'only' carrots and other veggie salads) for a long period of time, can trigger hair loss, though you may be thinking that you're consuming a healthy diet. Fortunately, stopping 'excess' vitamin A intake will reverse the problem.

Lastly, the following eating disorders can also lead to hair loss due to nutritional deficiencies they create in the body —

• **Anorexia:** Severe loss of appetite from irrational fear of gaining weight

• **Bulimia:** Overeating/binge eating, followed by inducing vomiting or taking laxatives to prevent weight gain.

Take a look at the chart (below) as to what nutrients you should bank upon for hair health, hair growth and their sources. Speak to your trichologist, if your diet appears to be adequate, but you continue to suffer from hair loss.

Nutrients	Role	Sources
Vitamin A	Prevents dryness of scalp by ensuring that body produces and controls enough supply of sebum, a natural oil required to keep scalp moist and healthy	Orange and yellow coloured fruits and vegetables like orange, sweet lime, papaya, mango; green leafy vegetables like spinach, fenugreek (*methi*) leaves, also drumstick
B-vitamins	Promote blood circulation in the scalp, hair growth; prevent premature greying, augment growth and repair of body tissues	Beans, peas, carrots, cauliflower, soybean, nutritional yeast, bran, nuts and eggs
Folic acid	Promotes hair growth by renewing the cells that grow hair. Its deficiency can lead to premature greying and hair loss	Beans and legumes, citrus fruits, wheat bran, whole grains, poultry, liver, green leafy vegetables

Biotin	Promotes healthy hair growth and protects against dryness. It also increases the elasticity of the hair's cortex, thus preventing breakage	Brewer's yeast, brown rice, green peas, lentils, oats, soybeans, sunflower seeds, walnuts, saltwater fish, egg yolk, milk, legumes and whole grains
Vitamin C	Aids in improving scalp circulation. It is important to maintain capillaries that carry blood to the follicles	Indian gooseberry (amla), guava, citrus fruits, pineapple, tomatoes and green peppers
Vitamin E	Increases oxygen uptake; this improves blood circulation to the scalp and growth of hair. Stimulates hair growth by enhancing the immune system	Nuts and legumes, wheat germ oil, soybeans, sunflower oil, safflower oil
Protein	Essential for hair growth. Amino acids created from proteins can have constructive effects on the look and feel of your hair	Lean meat; Pulses like whole moong dal, rajma, chickpeas (kabuli channa), soybeans; nuts, grains, soya, fish, eggs, dairy products
Copper	Essential for hair structure and pigmentation of hair	Mushrooms, spinach, sesame seeds, mustard greens, asparagus, cashews, peppermint, tomatoes, sunflower seeds, ginger, green, beans, potato
Zinc	Stimulates hair growth by enhancing immune function	Legumes and nuts
Iron	Important constituent of blood (haemoglobin); vital for adequate oxygenation of all tissues	Red meat, liver, fish, poultry, leafy vegetables, lentils, beans, dates
Selenium	Essential for normal thyroid function	Nuts, meat, eggs, fish, lobster, crab
Silica	Vital component of hair shaft, stimulates hair growth	Green beans, cucumber, celery, asparagus, mango, strawberries
Omega-3	Promotes a healthy scalp, regulates sebum production	Flaxseed, walnuts, cabbage, beans, broccoli, squash, fish oil, olive oil and salmon, sardines, tuna
Omega-6	Stimulates hair growth	Evening primrose oil, safflower oil, sunflower seeds, hemp seeds, corn and pumpkin seeds

SEASONAL HAIR CARE

SUMMER

Think of sweating without even doing the small stuff. This is summer for you.

The sweltering heat of summer sure drives many of us to exhaustion. It is also one of the primary triggers of various health issues and concerns — this is what that draws everyone to consulting the doctor.

What may, perhaps, not draw as much attention is the deleterious effects of summer on our scalp and hair.

The most obvious aspect of our body that is exposed to the hot summer sun's powerful (UV) rays is our hair. Blame it on one's occupation, or frenzied lifestyle, or think of what you may, the reality is the scorching heat of the sun often upsets the 'applecart' of our hair cuticles.

The result is **dry,** drab, brittle or **frizzy hair** and split ends.

Although the sun cannot actually 'burn' our hair, it can certainly affect its natural protective layer. Studies suggest that 3-4 days of protracted exposure to the sun would be enough to affect the scale-like cells covering the hair shaft to peel off. This is what makes our hair dry, dull, or brittle, and also fragile.

High levels of **humidity,** the bugbear of summer, also damage hair — humidity causes hair strands to stretch, while making them brittle.

*Top
Tips*

TOP 5 TIPS FOR HAIR CARE IN SUMMER

1. *Shampoo.* The heat of summer tends to wear out your hair's protective oils. Choose a shampoo that has natural active ingredients with minimal lather — this helps to minimise drying of hair. Combat loss of moisture on your scalp, a common dilemma during summer, with a mild moisturiser. Apply a natural conditioner after every hair wash, or whenever you wet your hair.

2. *Protect.* The sizzling wind that blows hot can wobble your hair. Wear a hat or carry an umbrella whenever you step out in the sun. Also, try and give your hair a break from the hair dryer during the summer months. If at all you would want to use the hair dryer, switch on a **cold blow**. Make sure to also keep the hair dryer at least six inches away from hair.

3. *Treat Dandruff.* Dandruff and excess oil on the scalp in summer are notable concerns. A daily hair wash with a mild, natural **anti-dandruff shampoo,** and a dab of **olive oil**, would be helpful to maintain healthy, natural hair.

4. *Swimming.* **Swimming may give immense relief** from the scorching heat of the sun in summer, but the chlorine in **swimming pools** is damaging to hair. Wear a **rubber cap,** when you are in the pool. Wash your hair with tap water, soon after swimming. This will help 'purge' chlorine from your hair.

5. *Nutrition.* Drink adequate water — at least one-and-a-half to two litres — everyday. This will help to flush out toxins. Diet is just as important — incorporate a good intake of **soy** and **sprouts** into your eating regimen. This is wholesome nourishment for your body and also for the 'soul' of your hair.

Summer need not be a hairy distress, or a season of unease — it can be a breeze, provided one incorporates the above tips and makes them a regular habit.

MONSOON

Many of us love to get wet in the rain. Rains are fun. But, they can also spoil our fun, or cause 'flooded' disruption to life.

Rains can rob your hair, your beauty emblem of its gloss, not to speak of undermining even the most ideal 'makeover' into a dampened disaster. Constant care is, therefore, just as much required, like any other time of the year.

Dandruff

Dandruff and hair fall are common maladies during monsoon. You may think it is futile to set, style, and reinvent your hairstyle, during the rains. This is not a good idea. It certainly makes sense to avoid that flat, damp or frizzy look, during the rainy season.

Top Tips

TOP 5 TIPS TO HELP YOU DEAL WITH MONSOON 'HAIR' BLUES

1. *Conditioning & Styling.* Hair conditioning and sporting a loose ponytail are good initiatives, because hair tangles easily during the wet season. Choose a mild shampoo that has natural active ingredients rather than lathering shampoos — the latter can make your hair frizzy.

2. *Shielding Your Tresses.* Avoid getting wet as floating pollutants/toxins can settle on your scalp, leading to hair loss. If you get drenched in the rain, wash your hair with a mild, natural shampoo, and follow it up with a conditioner — to keep the scalp free of germs.

3. *Pamper Yourself.* A relaxing therapeutic and rejuvenating head massage can revitalise damp hair roots and 'jazz-up' your hair.

4. *Protect Hair.* Use a scarf/cap to protect your hair from the wind and adverse damp conditions, especially while travelling by public transport. Oiling, with olive oil, and washing your hair, at least thrice a week, with lukewarm water is advisable. Towel-dry gently thereafter.

5. *Dandruff-fix.* If you have dandruff (a common occurrence during monsoon), use a mild anti-dandruff shampoo, enriched with the homeopathic *Thuja Occidentalis,* a natural anti-bacterial.

WINTER

When the cold winter waft blows on your face, you feel refreshed — more so, after 'sweating it out' over months of warm, humid weather.

However, the 'downside' is winter affects your hair and skin just as much as summer does — the fallout is a rough, itchy hair texture.

Your hair needs special care in winter.

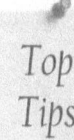

Top Tips

TOP 5 TIPS FOR HAIR CARE IN WINTER

1. *Head Massage.* As the winter steals away moisture from scalp, it leads to **dandruff** build-up and weakened hair follicles. Massage your scalp with warm olive oil to keep scalp problems at bay

2. *Shampoo Less Often.* Do not shampoo frequently as it can deplete the scalp of natural oils. You may shampoo hair twice a week. Use a mild shampoo and no matter how much you like hot water during winter, keep it away from your scalp. Wash hair with 'lukewarm' water

3. *Serum to the Rescue.* Choose a shampoo that has natural active ingredients; apply a serum or leave-in conditioner to lock the moisture in your tresses

4. *Put Away the Blow Dryer.* Hair gets dry and frizzy easily during winter. Don't add to its woes by blow drying hair. If you must, use 'cold blow' from a 'safe' distance

5. *Prevent Hair Breakage.* Hair breakage is common during winter; this can be controlled by using a wide-toothed comb, instead of hair brush. Drinking plenty of water keeps the body adequately hydrated and helps prevent hair breakage.

FOR 'HOLI-SAFE' HAIR

Holi, the festival of colours, is a wonderful occasion. It brings an array of colours — colours that paint our life bright.

Holi is a time to bond with family and friends. It is a celebration that both the young and old look forward to, with excitement. All of us enjoy the festival's revelry and review our festive success by the colourful remnants on our clothes and body.

Celebrations apart, most of us tend to ignore, or are unaware, of the potential damage the use of wrong colours can have on us. Some colours can be harmful to our hair; they can lead to more damage than delight.

It is imperative to be conscious of this possibility — we'd all do ourselves a huge favour by preventing any damage, at the outset.

Most colours today contain chemicals. Some also contain copper, lead, silver, aluminum and iodine. Hair would be the first to get affected badly following a splash of chemical colours. Also, chemicals not only bleach the hair, they can also damage the hair badly.

Certain chemical colours are tiny enough to penetrate the covering of our hair (cuticle) and enter the hair shaft. They can, thereafter, weaken the hair shaft, causing the hair to break easily.

Many individuals present with complaints of hair breakage, after Holi. This condition is called *trichorrhexis nodosa*.

Some colours contain dyes, engine oils, and powdered glass too! Apart from damaging the hair, they can also cause damage to the scalp. Some people show a dye 'reaction' to these colours too — this can cause long-term damage to hair and scalp.

Increased dandruff and itching of the scalp are other common complaints after Holi.

It isn't difficult to prevent such problems, if one follows certain easy-to-use preventative measures during Holi.

Oil is Well

Grandma was right, because oiling our hair never came in as handy as during Holi.

√ Oil forms a protective layer around the hair shaft

√ It prevents chemicals from entering the hair. It can also avert potential damage

√ Oil ensures that the colours are washed away easily

√ Oiling the hair before stepping out to play Holi would, therefore, be beneficial. Olive or coconut oil is ideal choice.

Use Natural Colours

It is best to use natural colours to play Holi. This won't cause any damage to others as well as to oneself. *Gulal* (rose water) and other natural water colours are relatively safe to use.

Chemical colours, particularly permanent colours, are best avoided. Colours, such as silver and shiny green or bright gold, are chemical-based; they should not be used.

Home-made colours from vegetable sources are safe. So, use —

√ Red sandalwood powder is a good substitute

√ Beetroot water is also a good wet colour

√ Dry spinach powder makes for a good green colour

√ Yellow turmeric (*haldi*) powder is a good natural yellow colour

✓ Dried marigold flowers and paste, or red hibiscus, can also be used as a substitute for artificial colour.

Natural colours can be used safely as dry powders, or mixed with water and diluted to be used as colours.

➡ Keep your eyes closed, when someone sprays, to avoid the colour from going into your eyes

➡ Wash your hair with lukewarm water — after playing Holi

➡ Use a mild shampoo and make sure to rub hair gently, and lather with shampoo.

➡ Rinse hair with lukewarm water. It would be advisable to repeat this process 2-3 times

➡ Follow this up by using a natural conditioner. The conditioner will soften the hair and prevent brittleness resulting from chemical colours

➡ Towel dry your hair lightly; avoid using a hair dryer

➡ Apply warm olive oil after your head bath

➡ It would be best to oil your hair for 2-3 days after Holi. Oiling the scalp will help keep your hair moist as well as soothe the scalp.

Remember, safety with colours can keep your hair glowing.

HAIR LOSS MYTHS

Common myths about hair relate to why and when it goes grey, what causes baldness, and how baldness can be prevented or treated. So long as people go bald, or are worried about going bald, myths about hair loss will always be around.

1. Mom's the Word: Is this A Question of Genetics

Baldness can come from either parent. One simple idea to foresee your own baldness is to look at balding patterns in your family. If you have your father, grandfather, an uncle who's bald or balding, all you need to do is ascertain when they began to lose, or lost their hair. This may provide you with some insights as to when you may also possibly go bald.

2. Washing Hair Everyday Keeps Hair from Re-Growing

Not really, if you use a mild, natural shampoo, while washing; it will actually nourish and add healthy moisture to your hair, instead of making it go dry.

3. Chop one grey hair, it will sprout a hundred

Not at all. Plucking one grey hair doesn't lead to a hundred grey hair nor does it encourage better hair growth.

4. Frequent Shampooing Causes Hair to Fall Out

Most people blame their shampoo when they see loose strands of hair in the bathtub, shower or sink. With the next shampoo session, they may just as well see more hair loss. This propels one's imagination — that shampooing causes baldness. Hereditary baldness is not caused by hair falling out, but by normal hair being slowly replaced by finer, thinner hair. Shampoo has got nothing to do with this cycle, or hair 'fall-out.' What's more, some people who don't shampoo their hair regularly feel they lose more hair when they shampoo — this happens because of build-up in the hair, which 'spurts' collective hair loss.

5. Oiling the Hair Makes it Grow Thicker and Longer

Hair oil, as your grandmother would define, is a great Indian tradition — for generations, natural hair oils have been praised as indispensable for healthy hair. Hair oil helps improve the texture of hair and aids in conditioning. But, as far as hair growth is concerned, this is governed by other factors, such as nutritional status, hormones and general health. Oil actually plays no role in hair growth.

6. Shaving the Head (*mundan*) makes a Child's Hair Grow Thicker and Faster

Mundan is a religious ceremony, in India, in which hair of the new-born is shaved off. The idea behind this ceremony is that hair of the new-born represents 'unwanted traits' from past lives. Hence, it must be shaved off to ensure a new beginning, a fresh start.

A lot of people believe that *mundan* makes the hair grow thicker and faster, but this is not true. The thickness and length of hair is pre-determined by your genes, not by rituals.

7. Rubbing Nails Controls Hair Loss and Helps Re-Growth of Hair

There is no scientific evidence to back this belief. Instead of losing time trying out such techniques, it is better to consult a trichologist who will diagnose the cause of your problem and provide you with the best possible solution.

8. Brushing Your Hair 100 Times a Day Makes it Grow Faster

Definitely not. Brushing helps to an extent by spreading the natural oils over the complete hair strand. Excessive brushing may only add to your hair woes; it damages hair due to excess friction.

9. No Visible Hair Loss Means No Balding

It's not necessary that you will go bald only if you notice hair visibly falling off. Sometimes, hair loss may not be obvious — in the form of hair on pillows or hair brush, in the drain or on the floor — yet you may keep progressing slowly towards baldness. This may happen because whatever hair is falling off is not being replaced by adequate new growth.

So, even if your hair is not falling off much, but you happen to notice reduced density of hair or hair thinning, remember, you may already be on your way towards balding.

10. Wearing Hats Causes Hair Loss

People think that wearing a cap or hat interrupts air circulation to the scalp and prevents the scalp from 'breathing.' This is not true. The reason being your hair follicles get their oxygen from the bloodstream, not the outside air. This only means that your hair does not 'choke,' if you wear a cap or hat — what's more, a golf cap, a popular option, hides your baldness. It does not show it.

What may actually trigger problems are caps or hats that fit tightly on the head. They may cause thinning around the sides of the head because of constant traction on the hair.

Wearing helmets for too long is also evidenced to cause traction alopecia, because the helmet rubs repetitively against a specific area of the scalp. All said and done, helmets are an absolute must for road safety; this cannot be compromised at any cost. One practical solution is to wear a bandanna underneath the helmet — this will reduce friction between the helmet and the scalp and save you from traction hair loss.

11. Standing on Head Improves Blood Flow and Reduces Hair Loss

Some people think that standing on one's head (or, performing the yoga posture, *sirsasana*) increases the blood flow to the scalp and improves hair re-growth or restoration. This 'upside-down' posture, propagated by yoga teachers and gurus, is a good yoga posture. There is, however, no real scientific validation or impact for the practice as regards hair loss or hair re-growth.

Growing hair also does require a considerable amount of blood flow, although decreased blood flow may sometimes lead to hair loss. Yet, reduced blood flow isn't the only cause for hair loss — it is the result of hair loss. Here's why — when good hair is placed into a bald scalp with decreased blood flow, the blood flow returns once hair starts to grow.

12. Magnets Increase Hair Growth

Proponents of magnetic therapy say that magnets can increase the blood flow to the scalp. This may help prevent hair loss or regenerate hair growth. This 'therapeutic' benefit has not been conclusively proved.

13. Hair Cuts Lead to Thicker Hair

This is not true. When you go for a haircut and cut your hair short, your hair gets scratchy like sandpaper. This gives us the feeling that our hair seems thicker than it was before. The actual fact is it is not thicker, it's just shorter. Hair, as you know, grows at a rate of half-inch per month. The rate does not change whether you cut hair daily, or opt for a haircut at long intervals.

14. Hair Loss Stops as You Get Older

Hair loss certainly slows down in men as they age. Men, after 60, see only marginal loss, if at all they have hair loss. For women, the reverse is true. With age and loss of oestrogen, the protective hormone, women (with genetic hair loss) find that their hair loss progression, which began during menopause, may increasingly worsen with age.

FREQUENTLY ASKED QUESTIONS

Your 'Hair-Raising' Questions Answered

1. Can My Hair Re-Grow? Will I Get back all the Hair I Have Lost?

This largely depends on the problem you have been diagnosed with and how far it has progressed. For example, male pattern baldness in its early stages responds well to treatment. In advanced stages, it may not be possible to bring back your lost hair but the progress of hair loss can be visibly slowed down. On the other hand, hair loss is 100 per cent reversible in most cases of patchy hair loss (alopecia areata), or after a bout of fever (typhoid, malaria), or anaemia. Hair loss is not reversible in scarring hair loss. It's best to consult a trichologist for a personalised review for each individual case.

2. How Long Will I Have to Take Treatment For Hair Loss?

Most cases of hair loss require long-term treatment (often for years) since the hair growth cycle itself is for 3-7 years. It is important not to lose patience during treatment because impatience and resulting stress will only slow down the process of recovery.

Consider it a lifestyle illness, much like high blood pressure or diabetes — you keep taking pills for all your life to keep them under control. This holds good for progressive hair loss — you may have to keep taking medicines for a long time, but then it's worth your time and effort.

3. Is Stress Related to Hair Loss?

There are about 40 different types of hair loss. Each type of hair loss has multiple reasons. Two or three types of hair loss are directly linked to stress — hair loss in patches **(alopecia areata)**, hair-pulling disorder **(trichotillomania)** and massive hair loss following an intensely stressful period (**telogen effluvium**) (*Read Chapter on 'Stress and Hair'*).

4. How Can One Control the Damage Caused by Hair Colours and Dyes?

Hair colours and dyes are harmful for your hair, but these have become a necessary 'evil' in our times. It is always better to do a patch skin test, if you are colouring or dyeing your hair to see if your skin reacts adversely. If your skin does not react, you can safely apply the colour or dye on the scalp. One good option is using a colour or dye with no ammonia. Coloured hair requires special care such as colour-protect shampoos, conditioning regularly, protecting from harsh sunlight, and washing with cool (at best, lukewarm) water.

5. Can Yogurt (Curd) and Beer as Some People Attest, Replace Branded Conditioners?

Not really, although yogurt (*dahi*) may, perforce, help in fighting dandruff, thanks to its probiotic ('good' bacteria) action.

Remember, hair loss and dandruff are primarily medical conditions. They are best treated by a professional trichologist, along with dietary changes.

A better, natural and healthier option in fighting dandruff is to 'up' the intake of flaxseed in your diet. Flaxseed has natural ingredients that help to control dandruff. Applying beer is a big 'no-no.'

6. What is the Role of Oils in Improving Hair Growth and as Conditioner?

Oil conditions your hair. So, if you have dry hair, applying oil is good, because it moistens hair roots and conditions your hair. Oil is also good for the scalp, but only if your scalp is dry. However, hair oil does not promote hair growth.

7. Is Henna a Good Option to Hair Dyes or Colours?

Natural henna is better than dyes and also safe — there are some scientific studies that support the view. While chemical colours seep into the hair shaft, henna only 'coats' the hair from the outside without seeping into the shaft. Hence, it is safe.

The only problem with henna is it dries up your hair. There is a trick. Just 'condition' your hair well before applying henna.

Henna does not promote hair growth; it has no effect on dandruff.

8. Is It Obligatory to Use Conditioners after Each Hair Wash?

A conditioner is good, once or twice a week; it softens your hair. But, you don't have to use it each time you shampoo your hair. A conditioner is useful if you have frizzy or dry hair. Some people use serum instead of conditioners. Serum has not been evaluated scientifically. Either way, it is better to use natural products to the best extent possible, like **Dr Batra's** Hair Conditioner.

9. What Makes a Good Hair Care Regimen?

Men must shampoo, thrice a week; women, twice a week, since they have long hair. Avoid the use of powerful, strong soaps on your hair. You may use a shampoo with natural extracts, and with good effect, too. Condition regularly, with a good conditioner. Oil, (preferably olive oil), may be applied regularly, along with a gentle head massage.

10. What is Your 'Best' Plan for Healthy, Lustrous and Beautiful Hair?

A calm attitude, good sleep, healthy relationships, balanced diet and a good hair care regimen.

Never abuse your hair with powerful colour treatments or 'amateur' parlour procedures that may cause damage to the hair.

Most importantly, the moment you notice hair loss, dandruff, or any other scalp problem, consult a professional trichologist — without delay.

Your hair will express a big 'thank you' for this.

CHOOSING THE RIGHT SHAMPOO

Walk into any cosmetic products showroom. It is likely that you will see a huge section allotted for shampoos. You may have dozens of shampoos, ranging from shampoos for dry hair, normal hair, oily hair; volumising shampoos, glossy, anti-dandruff, colour-protect shampoos, and many more.

Each product claims to be better than the other — each one

HAIR-FILE

- 80 per cent of people in the US wash their hair daily
- 90 per cent of Japanese wash hair daily
- Usage of shampoo in India is only once or twice a week
- A large percentage of Indians still use soap to wash hair
- Many Indians use henna and *shikakai* (soapnut powder) to wash their hair.

HAIR-FILE

The word 'shampoo' is derived from the Hindi word, *champoo*; its usage dates back to 1762.

Shampoos first originated during the Mughal Empire, where it was used for head massage — it consisted of alkalis, natural oils and other fragrances.

competing to find a place in your shopping basket and later in your bathroom.

How do you choose which one is the best for your hair? Is it the expensive one, or the one that claims to be natural, or is it the one that is mild and 'suits' even a baby's hair?

Top Tips

TOP 10 TIPS TO CHOOSE THE RIGHT SHAMPOO

1. Firstly, choose a shampoo that has natural active ingredients that are safer for scalp than chemicals

2. Select a shampoo that has been made for your hair type, depending on whether you have dry hair, oily hair or a combination

3. Ideally, your shampoo should have a pH close to 6.5, because this is the optimum pH of the scalp

4. Keep in mind that the amount of lather does not determine whether the shampoo is working or not. Actually, the less lather, the better, because it means that the molecules of the shampoo are grasping more dirt and oils

5. Coloured hair needs special care and protection from UV rays; there are special shampoos available in the market; if you have coloured hair, these have gentle cleansers

6. Choose an anti-dandruff shampoo, if you have dandruff or a greasy scalp. *Thuja Occidentalis* is a natural and proven anti-dandruff agent

7. For curly, coarse, frizzy hair, choose a creamy shampoo that tames the frizz — it helps to retain moisture in your hair

8. For fine hair that is limp or oily, choose a clear shampoo — one that is mild and can be used daily

9. For damaged or dry hair, use moisturising shampoos; they help to smoothen the hair and detangle easily

10. For chemically-treated hair (permed, straightened hair) use nourishing, creamy shampoos, since such hair is prone to damage and requires deep nutrition.

Top Tips

TOP 10 TIPS FOR YOUR CHILD'S HAIR CARE

1. Don't keep rubber bands in your child's hair during the night. This can damage the hair

2. Change hairstyles — a ponytail one day, braids the next, and then 'just let it loose' with a headband for a day or two

3. When working on knots, always start at the end of the hair; work towards the scalp, not in the other direction. Hold the hair between the ends and the scalp tightly in one hand as you comb the hair — the child will not feel the ache!

4. Use a plastic comb, not a brush

5. Never back-comb the hair; this will damage a child's delicate hair shafts

6. Allow your child to pursue interest in hair care; give them freedom for proper hair grooming

7. Examine your child's hair on a regular basis. This will help you to attend to hair lice — a common problem in school-going children

8. Use a mild conditioner to make the hair slide more easily when you're combing out the knots. For longer hair, use detangling agents along with a mild conditioner

9. Early detection and treatment is as important as prevention

10. Make hair care fun — also, an enjoyable experience.

Top Tips

TOP 10 TIPS TO WASH & DRY HAIR CORRECTLY

We all love our hair — this is reason enough to take good care of them, just like we do for all the precious things in life. Nurture them, pamper them and then flaunt them in style.

Use the **Top 10 Tips** to wash and dry your hair correctly — and, you will well be on the way to having healthy hair —

1. *Wash Your Hair with Lukewarm to Cold Water* — Twice a week for dry hair, thrice a week for normal hair and daily for very oily hair. Avoid hot water for hair, no matter how much you love it

2. *Shampoo Right.* Take a capful of shampoo on your palms and rub together. The best method of shampooing is to start with the scalp and roots and gently massage down along the shaft of the hair. Gently run fingers through the hair to make sure that the shampoo is evenly distributed, especially if you have thick hair. Rinse the shampoo by allowing the water to run from scalp to ends evenly

3. *Do Not Bunch or Squeeze Hair during Shampoo.* This could be damaging since hair is fragile when wet

4. *Rinsing.* As you rinse your hair, you should feel lighter and cleaner. If not, then shampoo and rinse again. Once the hair is rinsed thoroughly, you are ready to condition

5. *Conditioning.* Apply the conditioner evenly over hair strands while avoiding its contact with the scalp. Wait for a few minutes. Rinse well. Conditioner replaces the moisture in the hair shaft. It serves as a source of protein which temporarily attaches to the hair, protecting hair strands from breakage, while aiding detangling and manageability

6. *Drying.* Allow the hair to dry naturally. Avoid blow drying. A hair dryer releases gusts of 300^0F that causes hair to break. If you must use a dryer, use it on low-to-medium heat (better, cold) and hold it more than 6 inches away from hair

7. *Avoid vigorous rubbing.* Forceful rubbing with a towel is a big no, as this weakens hair roots, 'pulls out' hair and aggravates hair loss

8. *If You Want to Use Blow Dryer to Dry Your Hair.* Make sure to use it (cold) for not more than 4-5 minutes. Hold it at a distance of more than 6 inches from the scalp. Leave a little moisture on the hair in the end — do not burn out all the moisture

9. *Combing.* Never comb wet hair as hair is elastic when moist and can reach its breaking point easily. When hair is semi-dry or fully dried, use a wide-toothed comb. Avoid using a hair brush as it has a larger surface area; It can fracture the hair shaft. Wash your comb each time before you wash your hair to maintain scalp hygiene

10. *Oiling Before a Shampoo.* Hair oil acts as a moisturiser for the hair and scalp. It is advisable to apply oil at night before you shampoo the next morning. Avoid excessive oil application and keeping oil on for longer than for the night, as it attracts dust and grime, while rendering the hair difficult to clean.

Top Tips

TOP 10 TIPS FOR HEALTHY, GORGEOUS HAIR

Who would not love being complimented with a 'Wow; what lovely hair!'?

'Lovely hair' is not difficult, if you follow the **Top 10 Tips** given below. They will help you to nourish, pamper, groom, and protect your lovely locks and turn you into a head-turner — for the right reasons, of course!

1. *Trim Your Tresses in Time.* Yes, preferably every 3-4 months for women and every month for men. This will help to get rid of split ends and frizz and to give you the healthy look

2. *Comb Usage.* Use a wide-toothed comb to detangle hair. Avoid using thin-toothed combs since they damage the hair shaft

3. *Hair Accessories.* Hairpins, clips, and rubber bands can break the hair if used too tightly. If you want to use hairpins, use those with a smooth, ball-tipped surface. Hair clips should preferably have spongy rubber padding where they make contact with the hair. Rubber bands should be snag-free

4. *Get a Good Diet.* I've said enough about it earlier but I would like to say it again — nourish your body with a healthy, balanced diet rich in vitamins and minerals and watch your tresses shine with pride

5. *Screen From the Sun.* Prolonged exposure to UV rays can do significant damage to your hair — so, grab your umbrella or flaunt your hats and scarves whenever you step out in the sun

6. *Correct Usage of Appliances.* Blow dryers, hot irons and curlers are great to style your hair, but make sure you know how exactly to use them. If you don't know, avoid their use, rather than end up with burnt hair or the like

7. *Get Rid of Frizz.* Rubbing wet hair vigorously with a towel is one of the commonest reasons for frizzy hair. Pat your hair dry gently with a towel for best results

8. *Avoid Overuse of Styling Products.* It's great to style your hair on occasions but avoid overusing styling products — certainly not more than two products at any given time

9. *Space Out the Wash.* Unless you have extremely greasy hair, avoid washing hair everyday as it strips the hair of its natural oils and makes hair look dry, brittle and damaged. Determine the best frequency of hair wash in your case and stick to it

10. *Water-baby.* For all those who love swimming, do not forget to take a shower and rinse your hair properly after you get out of the pool, because chlorine in pool water can be damaging for hair.

I trust that you enjoyed reading this book,
just as much as I enjoyed writing it and
I hope this book will give you 'a breath of fresh hair.'

Dr BATRA'S HAIR SURVEY 2012

From my experience as trichologist, I have seen scores of people showing severe consequences of hair loss — in their professional as also personal lives. Besides, hair loss not only affects people psychologically and psychosocially, it also gives rise to inferiority complex, lowered self-esteem and depression.

This stirred me to take an 'inside look' into the minds of people — not necessarily hair loss patients — and, to find out how they feel about hair in general.

Nearly 4,000 people participated in the survey we conducted. The results, I believe, are worth sharing with my readers, because they illustrate the importance people bestow to their hair and also how far they would go to retain and take care of it — your crowning glory.

Take a *dekko*. Because, hair really matters!

Survey Results: Highlights

- A whopping 81% of women and 76% of men prefer alternative medicine for their hair loss as opposed to conventional medicine

- Over 70% of respondents believe bald men look 5-10 years older than their age

- As high as 70% of women understand that hair loss is a medical problem — and, correctly so!

- As high as 85% of all respondents believe that hair is the most important aspect of their appearance and over 80% feel that baldness would affect their self-esteem

- Interestingly, men spend a higher amount of money, every month, looking after their hair than women — some as high as INR 10,000!

Hair Survey Results 2012

#	Question	Female Respondents		Male Respondents	
		Yes	No	Yes	No
1	Are balding men less attractive to women?	75%	25%	78%	22%
2	If you started balding, would it affect your self-esteem?	85%	15%	79%	21%
3	Do men give preference to women with longer hair?	80%	20%	75%	25%
4	If you lost a lot of hair, would you be worried about how society perceives you?	74%	26%	68%	32%
5	Are balding men less preferred for jobs when compared to men with a head full of hair?	13%	87%	24%	76%
6	Do you think wigs look natural?	12%	88%	25%	75%
7	Would you opt for conventional treatment or alternative medicine, if you had hair loss?	Alternative 81%	Conventional 19%	Alternative 76%	Conventional 24%
8	How much money (in INR) do you spend in a year on hair loss treatment?	<5,000 62% · >10,000 11%	No Spend 26%	<5000 59% · >10,000 14%	No Spend 27%
9	Do you feel insecure about your appearance when you see someone with more healthy and beautiful hair?	Yes 79%	No 21%	Yes 76%	No 24%
10	Do bald men look older than their age?	No 18% · 5 Yrs Older 56% · 10 Yrs Older 20%	15 Yrs Older 6%	No 19% · 5 Yrs Older 53% · 10 Yrs Older 20%	15 yrs Older 8%
11	Is hair loss a cosmetic problem, or a medical problem?	Cosmetic 30%	Medical 70%	Cosmetic 42%	Medical 58%
12	Is hair the most important aspect of your appearance?	Yes 88%	No 12%	Yes 83%	No 17%
13	How much money (in INR) do you spend every month for looking after your hair (e.g., shampoo, beauty parlours, hair products etc..)?	<2,000 83% · up to 5,000 11% · up to 7,000 2%	up to 10,000 1% · >10,000 3%	<2000 80% · up to 5,000 11% · up to 7,000 3%	up to 10,000 3% · >10,000 4%

The Trichological Society, London

Dr Akshay Batra is —

- President – *The Trichological Society*, London, UK. He is the first ever non-Britisher to be elected President of The Trichological Society, a world-wide body of Hair Specialists and Hair Scientists

- Managing Director, *Dr Batras' Positive Health Clinic Pvt Ltd* — the first homeopathic healthcare corporate in the world — having over 100 speciality homeopathy clinics and having treated more than 2.5 lakh hair patients. Website: www.drbatras.com

- Director, *Dr Batra's B Perfect Clinics,* a chain of aesthetic day care clinics now in eight cities. Common procedures at B Perfect include hair transplantation, mesotherapy, weight loss treatments etc. Website: www.bperfect.co.in

- Director, *Dr Batra's Positive Health Products Ltd,* which manufactures FDA-approved natural hair products including natural shampoos, conditioner, hair oil, hair gel; skin care and lifestyle products. Website: www.products.drbatras.com

- Trustee, *Dr Batras' Positive Health Foundation,* a CSR-initiative, which treats over 20,000 patients free of charge, every year. Website: csr.drbatras.com

- Co-founder, *Dr Batra's Positive Health Awards* which honours specially-challenged individuals — who have demonstrated their indomitable will, by beating all odds to lead normal, healthy lives — every year. Link: youtube.com/drbatrasgroup.

Dr Akshay Batra may be contacted on the following platforms

E-mail: hair@drbatras.com

Facebook: facebook.com/akshay.batra.3154

Linkedin: linkedin.com/in/drakshaybatra

Twitter: twitter.com/drakshaybatra

Call Toll-Free #: 1800 209 2040